# The
# Divine Life

## Professor Hilton Hotema

ISBN: 978-1-63923-120-1

Printed: February 2022

Cover Art By: Paul Amid

Published and Distributed By:
Lushena Books
607 Country Club Drive, Unit E
Bensenville, IL 60106
www.lushenabks.com

ISBN: 978-1-63923-120-1

# The Divine Life

## *Table of Contents*

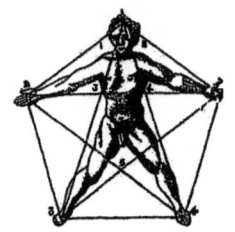

The Ancient Masters used the Pentacle to symbolize Man. He is constituted of Fire, Air, Water, Earth and Life. Two Pentacles were required to signify Birth and Death. The Black Pentacle fall of the Ego into Matter, Birth, and was called Crucifixion, due to confinement of the Ego in a prison. The Blazing Pentacle indicated release of the Ego from its prison by Death, and was termed Resurrection. The Masters said, "The day of (thy) Death (is better) than the day of one's Birth" *(Ecclesiastes 7:1)*. This is the esoteric meaning of the biblical statement, "Death is swallowed up in victory" *(1 Corinthians 15:54)*.

# Chapter No. 01
# What is Life?

The universe is full of mystery. In fact, if one should write a book on what is known, he would draft a new kind of textbook, a thin volume of few pages and of little value. He could begin thus:

"From science and by reason we as yet know neither whence the universe came nor where it is going; what I am that read this, nor what it is that I read, nor whether there is an I; nor what is energy or space or matter; nor the explanation of any force, or thing, or thought, or imagination, or love (Geoffrey Parsons, in Harper's Magazine)."

In *"The Book of Popular Science,"* which starts off by declaring that "science is remaking our lives," we read:

"What is life? Look about you and see people, animals and plants — all living. But the amount of life which is an unseen part of our environment is more multitudinous and universal, and influences our own lives as greatly as that which is seen.

"What is life? That is another question and the answer is one of the profound mysteries. Science has explored life down to a single cell of living matter, but exactly what makes that cell alive is not known." Later we shall see the absurdity of such phrases as "the amount of life," and "science has explored life down to a single cell of living matter." We shall see that man is lost because of his erroneous conception of Life. We shall see that the darkness in which man wanders, is due to the fact that he cannot find the Father, and that he becomes more hopelessly lost the more he searches.

From the remotest times men have attempted to raise the veil and penetrate the mystery of Life. Generation after generation of learned men have confidently advanced to attack the problem, feeling sure of victory, only to fall back, one after another, empty handed, baffled, defeated.

A famous "scientist," me time since, after giving the matter much study, tried to define Life. "Life," said he, "is a flame burning in water."

Ah, yes. Many thanks, sir. It is a beautiful definition; but the substance of it was known ages ago, when white-gowned Chaldeans paced their brick towers and meditated, under the Mesopotamian moon, on Life and Death, and the Universe. "A flame burning in water" — yes, but the flame was lighted eons and eons ago, a spark, maybe, struck off from some cosmic anvil, on which the "milky way" was hammered into shape:

Hippocrates, the so-called Father of Medicine, held to the doctrine that Life is "a flame burning in water." He considered heat not only the foundation of Life, but as the Divinity itself, intelligent and immortal.

Bichat opens his celebrated "Recherché Physiologiques surla Vie et la Mort," by defining Life as "the sum of the functions by which death is resisted." What does that tell us? Nothing. It is but a circuitous way of saying that Life consists in being able to live.

Doctor Fletcher says:

"Life consists in the sum of the characteristic actions of organized beings, performed in virtue of a specific susceptibility, acted upon by specific stimuli."

Richerand observes:

"Life consists in the aggregate of those phenomena which manifest themselves in succession for a limited time in organized beings." Herbert Spencer, who devotes the entire third part of his *Elements of Psychology* to a consideration of the question, brings us by slow and steady strides to the conclusion that:

"The broadest and most complete definition of life will be the continuous adjustment of internal relations to external relations."

The renowned Osier remarks:

"The studies of the physiologist and physiological chemist abundantly indicate that all vital activities are ultimately the expression of molecular rearrangements and combinations. Life is, therefore, the expression of a series of chemical changes, and the material endowed with life must be of such a nature that it, itself, is composed of molecules which react" (*Modern Medicine,* page 39, 1907).

Not one of these definitions explains what life is. They are but mere statements of certain signs of Life's; of the effects of Life; or the manifestation of Life in matter. If we are to understand by the word "Life" simply the attestations of its presence — the signs of Life nothing more — these authors have done as well, perhaps, as the subject permits.

How these and similar definitions fail to define what Life is, is further shown by asking what it is that produces the "state" and the "change" that are defined as Life. How can Life be defined as the state or changes of matter, when matter possesses no power of itself to produce the organized state, or to effect those changes, called Life?

It is reasoning in a circle to declare that Life is the change of state of matter, and that the change of state of matter is Life. We are in the same dilemma when we say that Life produces the activity of the brain, and the activity of the brain is Life.

The definition of Life must comprehend the thing attested; it must explain the CAUSE of the changes, or it is not a definition of Life, but only a description of the effects or manifestation of Life in Nature.

We seal a live man up in an air-tight iron safe, leave him there thirty minutes, then open the safe and find only an inanimate body. We say the man is dead. Why is he dead? What do we mean by "dead?" What has happened to stop the "continuous adjustment of internal relations to external relations," which "science" says is "Life?" Why does the process not begin again as soon as the safe is opened? What was there in or about the body when it was sealed up in the safe that is not there when the safe is opened? How could anything get out of the safe, made of iron, and sealed air-tight?

3

# Chapter No. 02
# The Dust of the Ground

God formed man of the dust of the ground *(Genesis 2:7).* In the sweat of thy face shalt thou eat bread, till thou return unto the ground; for out of it was thou taken: for dust thou art, and unto dust shalt thou return *(Genesis 3:19).*

Here we are twice told that man, yea, that the renowned scientist who would prove that the Creator is not, has a form composed of the shifting, despicable dust of the ground. We are further told that all flesh is as grass; that all the glory of man is as the flower of grass; and that the grass withered, and the flower thereof falleth away *(1 Peter 2:24).*

But vain man, in his pride and haughtiness, forgets that he is dust. He will not believe that his flesh is as grass; he will not have it that his glory is as the flower of grass, to wither and fall away as the petals of a dying pansy *(Psalms 103:15).*

Less than a generation ago little was definitely known of the substance, or chemical compounds, as they are called, entering into the composition of animal bodies. But materialistic science has made vast "progress" in recent years, and in knowledge as to this particular phase of human existence, has risen almost to the plane of the old Patriarch, and discovered by chemical analysis in the modern laboratory, that the human body is actually made of dust; that the chemical compounds of which it is composed, exist in the dust of the ground. Perchance this was a painful "discovery" for some scientists, who regard themselves as the product of a "special creation of refined star dust."

What did Moses know about chemistry? We have no reason to assume that he knew anything about chemistry. How did he know that the Creator "formed man of the dust of the ground?" How do we know that the Sun does not "rise?" Let us see.

From observation, the Sun, each day, appears to rise and set, and this information is carefully recorded in weather

4

reports and almanacs. By the same outward appearance man has been prone to judge all things, and on this foundation has based his philosophy.

Children and fools (men wise in worldly wisdom) live and die by appearances. They know nothing of that Truth which makes men free. They know nothing of the Life Eternal. They live in darkness, die in ignorance, and all their days they are slaves to their own fears and distorted imaginations.

The just shall live by faith *(Romans 1:17)*. That is the only way that men can live, and live right. Moses was not led astray by visible appearances. He gazed upon the body of man. The flesh and blood he saw did not resemble the dust of the ground. Yet his understanding told him that, since the body is developed, from the seed to maturity, and nourished all its days, by substances that come from the dust of the ground, the body of man, no less than the body of trees and plants, must be built up and composed of the dust of the ground. Time and science have proved that this is so.

Moses closed his eyes to visible things and used his understanding. Thus he discovered that the invisible things of Him from the creation of the world are clearly seen, being understood (thru faith) by the things that are made *(Romans 1:20)*. And now chat science has learned that the body of man is composed of the dust of the ground, this intelligence is accounted as an epoch-making discovery, and people are assured that science has made vast "progress."

Man then, as we know him, possesses a body formed of the dust of the ground. Regardless of what examination or test to which the body may be subjected, we can make nothing more out of it. This information may be almost as discouraging to some of the fine-blooded stock of the race, as to know that "the kingdom of God is within you."

# Chapter No. 3
# The Breath of Life

If it be possible, let us learn something about Life from the source that correctly informed the world, many centuries since, as to the constituents of the material part of man. After God formed man of the dust of the ground, He breathed into his nostrils the Breath of Life: and man became a living soul *(Genesis 2:7)*

The materialist was forced by investigation to accept as a fact, the first part of that statement: but as to the last part of it — well, Life is only "the expression of a series of chemical changes," a sort of "molecular re-arrangement and combinations," a "mode of motion." On that flimsy foundation materialistic science has erected its vast superstructure of labyrinth halls and passages, through which it continues to wander in perplexing confusion.

If science should now, or at any future time, recognize the animation of the animal body as being due to the direct effect of the *"Breath of Life,"* by that act it would destroy itself and all its worthless labor and love.

Consequently, while Time and Test have forced materialists to admit as truth, the statement that God formed man of the dust of the ground, they still reject as an unfounded myth, the existence of the *"Breath of Life,"* and have adopted in its place the make-shift theory that Life comes into existence as the result of the re-arrangement of a chemical formula.

This course the materialists have taken, because of their fixed stand not to believe in the Unseen Universe, or that such universe even exists.

The materialist lives on the visible plane, and will consider nothing that he cannot see, smell, feel, hear, taste, test, or demonstrate. Consequently, to him the great truths of the Unseen Universe, which can be comprehended only thorough faith, and never be fully explained by man, must remain forever an unsolved mystery. He must always remain a blind leader of those who follow him, and to him the *"Breath of Life"* is nothing more than a myth of antiquity.

The very "motion" or "chemical change," which the materialist observes and defines as Life, is but the effect of the *"Breath of Life"* acting on matter. But this he knows not, since he lives by sight, by appearances. He believes that beyond the range of telescope and microscope all is empty and void.

The difficulty of these men in clearly distinguishing between matter, motion, and force, is readily accounted for. Having perceived that certain forces are of too high and complex a character to be attributes of the grosser forms of matter, they could not attach them thereto. Having denied the existence of the *"Breath of Life,"* they are precluded from assigning them there. And perceiving that there cannot be visible activity apart from substance, they have concealed their errors in the only way left to them, viz., by ascribing Life to be the "continuous adjustment of internal relations to external relations."

Not only do materialists hold that Life is the "continuous adjustment of internal relations to external relations" of matter, but they go to the extreme of claiming that Life results from decomposition — from the stinking gas of rotting matter; from the lowest imaginable depths to the highest visible plane of existence.

Professor Le Conte observes:

"In all cases, vital (Life) force is produced by decomposition (*Conservation of Energy,"* etc., page 175).

On page 188 he again observes:

"Whence do animals derive their vital (Life) force? I answer, from the decomposition of their food and the decomposition of their tissues."

Science, where would you lead us if we should be so silly as to follow? Vital (Life) Force springs from matter in the process of decay! From decaying vegetables, from decaying animal tissues, comes forth Vital (Life) Force. The exalted, unlimited Force that builds mountains and moves worlds, that makes suns and moons and stars, that forms animals and endows them with numerous powers, that gives man an intellect by which he could raise himself far above the low level to which his miss-education has brought him — that Force is "produced by decomposition!"

Think of serious minded men, of so-called scientists, seriously defending such a preposterous proposition! What is there to look forward to in an education of our children, based on such wild speculation? No wonder that "science" is kept so busy explaining away its errors, and making so many "new discoveries" to hide its ignorance and confusion behind. If it's whole structure were dug up by the roots and cast into the sea, what a blessing it would be for humanity

Life, as we shall later see, is an intelligent, unseen force, that operates according to fixed laws in the production of definite, material forms, after positive patterns. It is not produced by the decomposition of matter; it does not originate in matter at all; it is not formed by or from matter; it is in no way dependent upon matter; and it is not capable of being converted into matter, with which it is, nevertheless, connected in some peculiar way, during the animated existence of plants, animals, and men.

Life is a power which we cannot isolate nor physically examine, but the effects of the action of which we may study (Professor L. S. Beale). Life . . . must have existed from all time, even when the globe was an incandescent mass, says Prayer.

Life always was. It had no beginning. But before Life could visibly express itself, so that man was able to perceive its presence, it had to construct matter into certain, definite, organized forms, through which to operate.

As Life functions through these physical forms, we observe the effect and mistake the effect for the cause, and say that these forms are alive. But we shall see that they are not alive. They are only the channels through which Life functions; and as soon as Life ceases to function through them, they become motionless, and dissolve back into the surrounding environment, out of which they were taken.

Before discussing further, the subject of Life, we must turn to other things, that a better understanding may be had of the subject at hand. To this end we shall notice next The Law of Creation.

# Chapter No. 04
# The Law of Creation

In the Bible it is written: In the beginning God created the heaven and the earth *(Genesis 1:1)*.

Then the story is related that God created everything from Earth to Man in six days, and "rested on the seventh day from all his work which he had made."

Moses, or a mythical figure dimly represented by that name, is generally accredited with being the author of this account of creation. Reverend Professor Sayce, of Oxford University, shows in his work, *The Higher Criticism and the Verdict of the Monuments*, that Genesis is a compilation of Babylonian legends, which the Jews had time to study and plagiarize during the Babylonian captivity.

Of this theory of creation George Henry Dole observes:

"The theory of creation by the fiat of the Almighty has failed to satisfy inquiring minds of deeper discernment. Law, order, and development are so related and conjoined, that the mind will not bring its searching's to an end, and rest its reasoning's in the belief that God, without the observance of laws as revealed in Nature, by word of mouth, called out of nothing the varied forms in the universe into existence" *(The Philosophy of Creation,* page 3).

Dole goes on to state that something cannot come from nothing, showing that the Creator must be a Substance, "the highest, purest, and primal substance of which law, quality, and force are attributes, and from which came matter with its attributes."

The Bible does not inform us what heaven and earth were created out of. There are some who assert that the world, with everything in it, was created out of nothing. On first thought this appears ridiculous and impossible; but a consideration of the question may shed more light on what we wish to know. Let us see.

Water is a substance that is visible to the human eye. It is formed by a combination of oxygen and hydrogen, under the influence of a phase of law called chemical affinity or cohesion. Before their combination, these two elements are invisible. At a certain temperature water becomes ice, a solid that will bear up the weight of elephants. By raising the temperature, the ice becomes fluid, and at a still higher temperature, the fluid decomposes and becomes a gas that is invisible to the eye. Are we correct in assuming that the oxygen and hydrogen are now nothing, merely because they cannot be seen?

The spiritualist says that matter has no existence. A rash statement we may think. But materialistic science has shown that matter has no visible, eternal existence — that matter is, in fact, as empty as the limitless sky.

What we know as matter is, in all probability, never visible until compounded. Anything that can be seen, however simple it may appear, is probably proved, by the very condition of its visibility, as being compounded.

Materialistic science claims that there are some 70 to 80 elements. Some hold that the actually primitive elements are probably only two; and this appears more reasonable. The two primitives, man may never see. No one has seen oxygen, hydrogen, or nitrogen, yet almost 85 per cent of the human body is composed of these invisible gases. In fact, oxygen alone makes up about half the entire matter composing the earth. Rocks are nearly one-half oxygen.

Matter comes into visible existence through the formation of invisible elements into visible compounds under the influence of cohesion. What is cohesion? We might as well ask what is gravity, atomicity, electricity, capillarity. Cohesion is nothing in or of itself. It is merely tangible evidence that back of all, is an Omnipotent Creative Force. Let the influence of cohesion be annulled by the withdrawal of the sustaining energy, no longer impelling the constituent oxygen and hydrogen to combine, and every drop of water on earth would instantly decompose and disappear.

Under a similar withdrawal of the sustaining energy of Creative Force, every compound, solid or fluid of nature, would instantly decompose and disappear. Yea, as massive and impregnable as this great globe appears, even it would dissolve into thin air and a little metallic matter. Nor is that all. Just as water is resolvable into the invisible elements of oxygen and hydrogen, so those matter, in all probability, along with the metals, phosphorus, iodine, etc., are resolvable into yet finer elements, into which, unless supported by sustaining energy, they would similarly decompose and disappear.

If Life is "the expression of a series of chemical changes," or the "continuous adjustment of internal relations to external relations" of matter, what becomes of Life when these changes and relations are disrupted and come to an end with the end of matter. No doubt it just floats off aimlessly into space, like a cloud of dust or smoke.

But matter does not end. Those who so believe, live by sight. The end is only apparent, not real. Matter has merely been reduced from visibility to invisibility. It still is, although in an invisible state. Under certain conditions, it will re-appear and become visible, just as ice, first becomes water, then gas and disappears from view, only to re-appear again in drops from the clouds above, which swell the rivers and flood the lands.

In this we behold the truth of the saying that is written: The invisible things of Him from the creation of the world are clearly seen, being understood by the things that are made (visible). All visible things must and do exist in an invisible state, or else nothing visible could be made to appear.

Men believe, because they are so taught, that the process of creation was a primary act of the Creator, performed ages ago. How sadly do they miss the truth? The process of creation has been going on with endless regularity since the law of cohesion first began to operate, and it will continue for all time to come.

The sparkling drops of water that fall today from the lowering clouds, are composed of the same water that bore the barks of the conquering Romans to the shores of fated Carthage; and that water is the same as the water which floated the Ark of Noah to its resting place upon the mountain of Ararat *(Genesis 8:4)*. And the foaming billows that kissed the prow of Noah's Ark, were composed of the same waters, upon the face of which the Great Spirit of the Universe moved (brooded) *(Genesis 1:2)*.

It is an ignorantly constructed theology that regards the Creative Force as having created only in past ages, and then departed and left the world to its fate. For the process of creation is occurring under our very nose, yet we know it not because of our miss-education regarding the manner in which it takes place.

Just as the animal body is constantly being broken down and re-constructed, so is every department of the visible being constantly broken down and re-built. In the rising sun, the falling rain, the changing clouds, the growing vegetation, and developing animal bodies, the work of the Creative Forces is exhibited no less palpably now, than at any time in the realm preceding ages.

The Creative Force, through the law of cohesion, is constantly bringing together the invisible gases of the unseen universe, and constructing them into visible compounds, and weaving these compounds into mineral, vegetal, and animal forms, through which the Divine Life expresses itself, corresponding in kind of expression, not to the "kind of life," as some authors assert, but to the kind of form through which the expression occurs.

How close we are brought to the Creative Forces, thus to regard that Force not so much as having made the world and all it contains, but as still engaged in making and re-making it.

This brings us to "The Law of Change," which shows more clearly how the work of creation is conducted.

# **Chapter No. 05**
# **The Law Of Change**

Nothing is permanent but change. We have often heard that remark; yet how little it has meant to us. We did not give it a second thought. But herein lies the solution of a problem that has puzzled man from the beginning. For the eternal change of substance that is continually occurring has been going on since "God created the heaven and the earth," and will continue in its uninterrupted course until Time is no more. It cannot stop, for it is the Law of Creation, merely stated in another way, and if it ceased for a second, all things would come to a sudden end.

From the invisible substance of the Universe, visible forms, under the law of cohesion, come into existence. They remain visible so long as they conform to the phase of the law that makes them visible, and are returned to the invisible state — the store-house of building material — when they cease to conform to the phase of law that brings them into visibility. Since water is the most-simple compound, it is the best example of this constant change from visibility to invisibility.

While in the visible state, all forms are constantly undergoing change. The Law Of Change — the law of creation — is always at work. At no time are visible forms completely composed of the same material, of which they were composed a moment before. It is and must be, however, the same kind of material, but not the same material. As soon as the material becomes changed in kind, in that moment the law of *"each after its kind"* is violated, and that particular form begins to disintegrate and decay, as a result of such violation.

A river is a splendid illustration of the law of change. Down through the ages it lies upon the landscape, with size, length, breadth, seeming solidity, and seeming permanency. It remains throughout the centuries, apparently fixed and unchanging; yet at no time is it composed of the same water that composed it a moment before. Its waters are constantly changing, in relation to its bank and bed, along the whole course, from its source, to its mouth; and the time comes, at certain and positive intervals, when the water is completely changed from one end of the course to the other.

The water is leaving the bed of the river by flowing into the trackless ocean, by evaporation, and by exosmosis. New water must be supplied, and in the same ratio as the old water leaves the river. Failing in this, a time will come when there will be no river. And also the river will disappear if sawdust or sand be supplied instead of water. The river depends for its existence upon a certain kind of material. A violation of this law means disappearance of the river.

The animal body is no exception to the law of change. The change that goes on in streams of water, is just as incessantly going on in animal bodies. Through the process of destruction and construction, the animal body is torn down and rebuilt, particle by particle, cell by cell, tissue by tissue. In fact, the sole and final object of all body function is to maintain the integrity of the organism; and this is accomplished by the law of change.

All matter is subject to the law of disintegration and decay. Material forms must be constantly renewed, or they lose their stability and integrity, and dissolve into invisible vapors and gases. It is through the process of destruction and construction — the law of change — that material forms, animals and men, are maintained in a visible state.

Animal bodies cannot defy this law. In order to exist as such, these bodies must meet the requirements of the law by constantly undergoing the process of change. Physically, no part of our body is the same now as it was an hour ago; and some physiologists and biologists have estimated, that within a year the human body is completely destroyed, and rebuilt of new material, down to the largest and hardest bony structure.

The body we have today is not the body, as to its material, that we had a year ago. It is the same body in appearance and pattern, but not in material. It is and must be of the same kind of material, but not of the same material. As soon as the material becomes changed in kind, as we have said, the body at once begins to decay more rapidly than it is and can be renewed. This in time means the end of the body.

The reason why bodies deteriorate and go down to dust, is because the kind of building material that their owners furnish them, is not the kind that is suitable to repair their wasting parts, and sustain them in health. Animal bodies exist just as long as they are able to survive on the kind of material that they must use to re-construct their disintegrating parts. But we must not anticipate. This phase of the subject shall be more fully discussed in another place.

The materialist, not understanding the law of change, says that matter is; and he is right. The spiritualist, not understanding the law, declares that matter is not; and he also is right. The controversy arises from the fact that the materialist believes in the existence of visible matter, but not of invisible substance, while the spiritualist believes only in the existence of an invisible spirit.

The materialist holds that Life is "the expression of a series of chemical changes" occurring in matter; and if that were true, we could never get Life into existence. The spiritualist holds that matter does not exist, that all is Spirit; and if that were true, we could never see the expression of Life, since it would have no visible forms through which to make its presence known.

Down thru the ages these two schools have argued, quarreled, and fought, each getting nowhere and solving nothing. But human thought through both of these channels has continued to roll onward, through the years of speculation into the sea of doubt.

Having observed that out of the invisible comes the visible, what shall we say to those bigoted men who hold that the world, with everything in it, was created out of nothing?

How shall we ever be able to reach their closed understanding and teach them that something from nothing is impossibility?

And what shall we say to the dogmatic ones who hold that, since plants, animals, and men decay and die, and even the rocks disintegrate, a time will come when the earth will dissolve and disappear? We shall answer them that, the crumbling material forms do not foretell the final dissolution of visible things; but, on the other hand, when rightly viewed, they reveal to us that the visible plane is the workshop in which puny man becomes cognizant of the manner in which the Creator works.

The earth is the plane where the visible, constructive operation of the Divine Life forms and reforms the machinery through which it operates, thus preserving and perpetuating the channels through which it works.

# Chapter No. 06
# The Creative Force

To acquire some knowledge of the Creative Force, we must pass beyond the range of human vision, and be guided by faith instead of by sight.

Some think that the Creative Force is an Omnipresent Force. It could not be otherwise, for in the absence of this Force from any department, that department would immediately decompose and disappear, as we have observed.

We must also remember that Force cannot exist apart from an embodying substance. But that substance can exist without being perceived on the visible plane, as we have seen.

In fact, Force, in order to operate, must have channels through which to function, and these channels must be composed of substance. To that extent we may say that Force and substance are inseparable. We know nothing of Force except through the media of substance, and but for substance, the existence of Force would be unknown, and we would be not. We should not understand the term "substance" as applying only to visible matter that can be seen and handled, for we have observed that substance also exists in an invisible state. That is why Life can function on both the visible and the invisible plane; since wherever Life is received, whether in the material (visible) world, or in the spiritual (invisible) world, there is and must needs be substance to receive it.

The invisible substances are none the less real, because they are beyond the reach of the eye, or of chemical analysis. Indeed, it is only the grosser expressions of substance, or matter, that the senses can apprehend. As for invisibility, which to those who live by sight is proof of non-existence, no warning is so incessantly addressed to us, from every department of the Universe, as not to fall into the error of disbelieving simply because of not seeing. We are constantly admonished to have faith in order to solve the problems which appear, to our sight, as perplexing and confusing.

By faith, not by sight, we understand that the words were framed by the power of the Great Spirit of the Universe, so that things which are seen were not made of things which do appear *(Hebrews 11:3)*. In other words, we are to understand that things which are made visible, declare the invisible things that were not made visible. And that which we see going on about us every day, declare that which has taken place from the beginning.

The derivation of the visible world from an anterior, invisible world, is expressly taught in the Scriptures:

"These are the generations of the heavens and of the earth, and every plant of the field before it was in the earth, and every herb of the field before it grew" *(Genesis 2:4, 5)*.

These words, says Philo Jadeus:

"Do manifestly teach that, before the earth was green, verdure already existed; that before the grass sprang up in the field, there was grass, though it was not visible. The same must we understand from Moses in the case of everything else which is perceived by the external senses; there were elder forms and motions already existing, according to which the others were fashioned and measured out. The things that he (Moses) has mentioned are examples of the nature of all."

The spiritualist may seem mad to the materialist — and mad he is, if merely a spiritualist. But how much more-sane is the so-called scientist, who believes that nothing worthwhile exists, if it lies beyond the range of the telescope or microscope?

The Creative Force is the Power that lies back of all things, visible or invisible, and is the cause of all that occurs. What that Force is, no man will ever know, but this much we do know: The Creative Force is the efficient and sufficient equal of all that has taken place, all that can take place, and all that ever will take place.

# Chapter No. 07
# Origin of Life

The eternal error that has enslaved the race, has been the crude, materialistic, scientific conception of Life. Instead of Life coming from the highest, and being the prime mover, science reverses the process, and has Life springing from the lowest.

Instead of Life being an Intelligent, Infinite Force, flowing from the Creative Energy, and constructing matter into definite forms through which to express itself, Life, says science, is the result of a chemical compound, and when the compound disintegrates, "life" comes to an end.

Indeed, Professor Le Conte would go lower than this for the source of Life, for he says:

"In all cases, vital force (life) is produced by decomposition." Will you think of that? Out of the fumes of decaying matter, the lowest state that we can conceive, comes forth the Flame of Life, the highest known state of existence — the brilliant beam that pierces all things, animates all things, and performs all conduct and function, and yet so subtle that no man can "tell whence it cometh), and whither it goeth" *(John 3:8).*

All "life," according to science, originated millions of years ago, long before the dawn of man, in the warm waters of prehistoric seas. Down in the dark depths of the ancient oceans, "life" accidentally came into existence by a chance combination of particles of slime, which, upon combining, set up a chemical reaction that generated THE FLAME OF LIFE BURNING IN WATER.

Moses made a wild guess when he stated, that the Breath Of Life from the Creator made of man a "living soul;" and

Christ referred to fumes rising from a combination of homogeneous slime when he said:

"The words that I speak to you, they are spirit, and they are life" *(John 7:63)*.

Since we have the difficult part of our task performed, since we have so easily brought "life" into existence, it should be easy for us to explain the origin of all the various living forms. By simply falling back on the popular theory of the Materialist and the Evolutionist, we can have these particles of decomposing slime gradually assume definite form, and after evolving through many and diverse stages, each one rising successively to a higher plane, can develop the decomposing slime into a backboned fish — the "father of the vertebrates." And now what happens?

Ages come and go. The fishes multiply and grow restless in the darkness of the deep, and some begin to come out into shallow water along the shore, searching for new scenes and pastures. A tidal wave conveniently comes along and washes these into shallows where they are left by the receding water. As the water dries up, the fish must either die or learn to breathe the heavy air of those prehistoric days. They chose the latter course — for who likes to die?

Finding themselves on dry land, and growing hungry, they must either starve to death or learn a new mode of travel. So by great effort they learn to crawl about among the plants that bordered the waters of their remote world. Some of the more ambitious decide to walk instead of crawl, and these flop about on their fins, made only for swimming. After thus laboring for many ages, the fins gradually evolve into feet.

Observe, dear reader, that as we develop the "scientific" theory of evolution, we must ignore the law "each after its kind." No one has ever known this law to be violated, and no exception to it has ever been found. But we cannot evolve slime into life, and fishes into men, without disregarding all law and order, for if it is done at all, it must be done in defiance of law and order.

Continuing the story. It happened that some of the more ambitious of the legged fishes found that it would be advantageous for them, in search of food, to climb bushes and trees, on which grew the luscious fruits. It was further found that time and trouble expended in climbing up and down trees, could be saved by leaping from branch to branch, and from tree to tree. This exercise was useful in developing legs, especially the hind legs. The leaping later began to develop the fore legs into wings; and as the fishes took to flying, the hind legs of this class began to atrophy as the wings, by constant use, took on greater development.

As time passed and development proceeded, some of the fishes found that they could stand erect and move about with great facility on their hind legs alone. The constant repetition of this attitude by this class slowly changed the hind legs and skeleton, until finally the two-legged gait in the erect posture became easy and comfortable.

To make a long story short, the process of "evolution" continued, slowly no doubt, until in time the monkey family evolved into existence, and finally man — the materialist, the spiritualist, the ruler, the king.

And here stands man, erect in all his self-made glory; despising his lowly origin; denying the truth of Life; contending that he is Life — the product of a special evolution; and holding that there is in store for him greater things than tongue can tell or pen portray — Life Eternal in a heavenly home.

He is Life, says he, by virtue of chemical reactions occurring within his body. He exists, he claims, not by virtue of law, but in spite of law, against the influence of which he has had to struggle in order to develop his body, from its inception in the particles of slime, to its present perfect state.

Man did not receive life. Life is a force generated by a chemical compound. Man did not receive a body. He was compelled to develop it. His body did not receive fins when he was a fish; he developed these in his effort to swim, just as he later developed his fins into feet in his effort to walk on land. In other words, man has struggled with Nature and wrested from her all that he has.

Nature has yielded to the demands of man because she lacked power to deny them. Man believes that he is, not by virtue of the law, but in spite of the law; and as such, he absolutely refuses to believe that there is any law which regulates his conduct in relation to his environment. But this phase of the subject shall receive due consideration in another place.

This is the absurd theory of the origin of Life, on which is based all modern educational systems, including theology and medicine. The accepted religious opinion is, that Soul and Man, in a manner unknown, unite for a time, then Life goes to the grave in death, to be resurrected at some indefinite future date, in a manner also unknown, and go through another state of existence.

We shall see that the Life about which we write, and which is all the Life there is, is something far more than the result of chemical reaction. We shall further see that man is not alive, much less being Life; and that the Life of which we speak, never dies.

# Chapter No. 08
# Kinds of Life

In the preceding chapter we have briefly related the origin of "life" from the scientific standpoint, showing that "life" originated in the waters of the salty seas. We also saw how, by virtue of the desire of the animal, and not the voluntary consent of Nature, the animal was able, by its own efforts, to develop from one species into another. The law of "each after their kind" was disregarded. It did not enter into the proposition at all. In fact, in the eyes of science, law exists in fancy, but not in fact.

In discussing the subject of Life, writers are prone to mention the various "forms" of "life," such as plant life, bird life, animal life, and so on. Professor Henry Drummond believes in the various "forms of life," and cites the Bible to support his belief. He says:

"There are a great many different kinds of Life. If one might give the broader meaning of the words of the apostle: 'ALL life is not the same life. There is one kind of life of men, another life of beasts, another of fishes, and another of birds.' There is the Life, or the Artist, or the Potter who segments the worm, the potter who forms the dog, the potter who moulds the man.

"What goes on then in the animal kingdom is this — the Bird-Life seizes upon the bird-germ and builds it up into a bird, the image of itself. The Reptile-Life seizes upon another germinal speck, assimilates surrounding matter, and fashions is into a reptile." (*Natural Law In The Spiritual World* page 292).

The inconsistent part of the proposition is, while there are many different "kinds of life," and a different "potter" that moulds the different "kinds of life," all "kinds of life" come from one kind of material — one clay. Drummond observes:

"Take the ovule of the worm, the eagle, the elephant, and of man himself. Let the most skilled observer apply the most searching tests to distinguish one from the other and he will fail. But there is something more surprising still. Compare next the two sets of germs, the vegetable and the animal. And there is still no shade of difference. Oak and palm, worm and man all start in life together. No matter into what strangely different forms they may afterwards develop, no matter whether they are to live on sea or land, creep or fly, swim or walk, think or vegetate, in the embryo, as it first meets the eye of Science, they are indistinguishable."

The human potter, from one kind of clay, moulds with proficiency and skill anything and everything, from plants to peacocks, from monkey to man, from men to angels, from angels to gods, according to a certain and definite plan. But the Infinite Potter, being less adept and skillful than the finite potter, is incapable of doing this; so there "must in short be as many potters as there are forms," says Drummond.

Why does he hold to this view? There is a purpose back of it, and we soon find it. Here it is:

"There is another kind of Life of which Science as yet has taken little cognizance. It obeys the same laws. It builds up an organism into its own form. It is the Christ-Life. As the Bird-Life builds up a bird, the image of itself, so the Christ-Life builds up a Christ, the image of Himself, in the inward nature of man. When a man becomes a Christian the natural process is this: The living Christ enters into his soul. Development begins. The quickening Life seizes upon the soul, assimilates surrounding elements, and begins to fashion it."

Here is a typical illustration of the astute manner in which writers and authors turn, twist, and juggle words, in order to fabricate support for their absurd theories and philosophies. Man deliberately shuts his eyes to truth in order not to believe, that the same phase of Divine Life which animates his form of clay, is the same which animates the forms of the bat, baboon, and bobcat, the jack-rabbit, jackal, and jackass. Drummond will not have it, that the same phase of Divine Life which animates his material form is the same which animated the material form of the subtle serpent of the Garden of Eden.

Wood, the Naturalist, in the preface to his great work in three volumes, concludes with these words:

"Every being which draws the breath of life, forms part of one universal family, bound together by the ties of a common creature-hood — and as being ourselves. Members of that living and breathing family, we learn to view with dearer eyes and more reverent hearts those beings which, although less Godlike than ourselves in their physical and moral natures, demand for that very reason our kindliest sympathies and most indulgent care. For we, being made in the image of God, are to them the visible representations of that Divine Being who gave the Sabbath alike for men and beast, and who takes even the sparrows under His personal protection.

"It is a great thing to be acquainted with the material framework of any creature, but is a far greater thing to know something of the principle which gave animation to that structure."

These are the conclusions of a man who spent his life in the study of the lives and habits of animals; and this was written in 1853, in the day when the study of the living creatures about him inspired a simple piety in the heart of the great naturalist, and led him to see that "every being which draws the breath of life, forms part of one universal family, bound together by the ties of a common creature-hood."

If we shall believe that God is omnipotence, omniscience, and omnipresence, and that God is Divine Life, we must also believe that Divine Life animates not only man, but everything that liveth. This is the doctrine that Giordano Bruno taught in the latter part of the sixteenth century, and for his pains the priesthood burned him on the pyre in February, 1600. In his last moments an idolatrous monk thrust a crucifix through the blaze to the burning man, but the dying martyr turned his head away, more in pity at such ignorance than in aversion at the offer.

"God," said Bruno, "is in every blade of grass, in every grain of sand, and in every atom that floats in the sunshine." But "the vulgar creeds of religious bodies have not dared to reveal the Truth in its purity and essence."

Bruno observes further:

"Rather would the Church cover the truth with allegories, with myths and mysteries, which they call sacred; and humanity adorning the veil, failed to lift itself up to see the idea behind it. Men saw through the teachings of the Church the shadow rather than the light."

The reason that religionists burn men for holding such beliefs and making such declarations, is that it brings man down, in that respect, to a level with the beasts of the field. "It might guarantee the Immortality of every living thing," observes Drummond. He continues:

"In the dog, for instance, the material framework giving way at death, might leave the released canine spirit still free to inhabit the old Environment. And so with every creature which had ever established a conscious relation with surrounding things.

"Now the difficulty in framing a theory of Eternal Life, has been to construct one which will exclude the brute creation, drawing the line rigidly at man, or at least somewhere within the human race."

Man associates with the animal creation here on earth, and makes beasts of burden of many of them. His progress, of which he is so proud, would have been vastly retarded, but for the friendly aid and assistance of the faithful horse. Still, in building a "theory of Eternal Life," he considers none that does not "exclude the brute creation," and crucifies and burns men who are so bold as to assert, that Divine Life is God, and that every form results from the indwelling of the Divine Life.

What a terrible disappointment it would be for the fanatical religionists, those super-spiritualists who rejoice in burning men to please their personal God, to find, when their small, selfish "soul" enters the "heaven" they have dreamed of in their material way, that centuries before the "souls" of the prehistoric beasts had preceded them to this blissful place.

Solomon cannot be included in this class. He believed that all forms were animated by Divine Life, and that, to this extent, man had no preeminence above the beast. He said:

"I said in mine heart concerning the estate of the sons of men, that God might manifest them, and that they might see that they themselves are beasts.

"For that which befalleth the sons of men befalleth beasts; even one thing befalleth them: as the one dieth, so dieth the other; yea, they have all one breath; so that a man hath no preeminence above a beast; for all is vanity. All go unto one place; all are of the dust, and all turn to dust again.

"Who knoweth the spirit of man that goeth upward, and the spirit of the beast that goeth downward to the earth?" *(Ecclesiastes. 3:18-21).*

Man is related to everything in his entire environment — the beasts, the birds, the reptile, the fish, and finally and fundamentally, to the plant, the base from which every animal form derives its material substance. The form through which Divine Life expresses itself may be a worm, a frog, a dog, a monkey, or a man, but it is, nevertheless, an expression of the One Animating Force of the Universe.

Doctor H. Meadow's remarks:

"Although there is no fundamental difference between the lowest and the highest expression of life, we find a higher elaboration of basic principle the higher we ascend in the scale of life. The process of digestion, for example, is basically the same throughout nature. It consists in the reduction of the same substance of which the creature is composed, by a chemical process, to a liquid condition in which is can be utilized by the organism. An increase in complexity is the only difference between the higher and lower Creature. This same law holds good anatomically, functionally and mentally throughout nature."

Those who are too weak to take their life and build a Christ, lull themselves into blissful ignorance by thinking that this will be done for them by a Christ-Life. But truth does not change because it is not believed. Our thoughts change us, but not the things about which we think.

"The words that I speak to you," said Christ, "they are spirit and they are life (truth)." And from this time on many of his disciples turned from him, and walked no more with him *(John 6:63-66)*. Man thinks that he is searching for truth. He accepts everything but truth, and truth alone he rejects, while he burns and crucifies the Servants of Truth.

Life does not build up a Christ. Life builds forms — not forms of Life but forms of minerals, vegetables, and animals. Life, the invisible force, builds visible forms through which to express itself on the visible plane. And it is the kind of form that determines the "kind of expression" which Life will manifest through that form.

Reptile-Life and Bird-Life is Divine Life expressed through those forms. Human-Life is Divine Life expressed through the human-form. Christ-Life is Divine Life expressed through the human-form that deports and conducts itself in a Christly way.

In the face of this truth, which none can dodge, we may weep with Solomon:

For in much wisdom is much grief: and he that increaseth knowledge increaseth sorrow *(Ecclesiastes 1:18)*.

# Chapter No. 09
# The Hidden Artist

In trying to solve the mystery of what Life is, science, we have seen, has traced the path of Life down to the smallest visible particle of matter, and there found no more to explain what Life is, than is found in a living man.

It is the spirit that quickeneth; the flesh profited nothing *(John 6:63)*. According to the Scriptures, the expression "Breath of Life," "Living Soul," "God," and "Spirit," are all interchangeable terms, each having the same meaning, each referring to the same thing. The word "spirit" is derived from the Greek "spiritus," meaning "breath." So when we speak of the "spiritual world," we refer to the "breath world," whence comes the "breath of life" into the natural world (G. H. Dole, *The Philosophy of Creation*, page 122).

In his *Psycho-Bio-Physiology*, Doctor Willard Carver observes:

"All things indigenous to the earth, are in themselves inanimate, and only take on conduct of animation when they are impelled in a specific way by the Force of Life. Things that move in the conduct which we call animation, are not alive. Life is imminent in such structures, but not inherent in them (page 167). Life, as it is observed in this material existence, is but the action of matter under the operation of force" (page 179).

We have seen that the substance from which the form of man first begins, is indistinguishable from that which enters into the beginning of the oak, worm, eagle, or elephant. This material is "a clear structure-less, jelly-like substance resembling the albumen or white of egg." Of this Professor Lionel S. Beale says:

"There is, indeed, a period in the development of every tissue of every living thing known to us, when there are actually no structural peculiarities whatever — when the whole organism consists of transparent, structure less, semi-fluid bioplasm — when it would not be possible to distinguish the growing moving matter which was to evolve the oak, from that which was the germ of a vertebrate animal. Nor can any difference be discerned between the bioplasm matter of the lowest, simplest, epithelial scale of man's organism, and that from which the nerve cells of his brain are to be evolved. Neither by studying bioplasm under the microscope nor by any kind of physical or chemical investigation known, can we forms any notion of the nature of the substance which is to be formed by the bioplasm, or what will be the ordinary result of the living."

Starting in the uterus of the female, in this clear, structure-less colloid, an unseen and mysterious something, called the Potter, begins to perform certain conduct. No science can define it. No eye can see it. If examined under the highest powers of the microscope, nothing can be distinguished but the clear, structure-less colloid. What is this invisible something? Drummond says:

"The Artist who operates upon matter in this subtle way and carries out his law — is Life."

Thus we observe that Life is subjective, while matter is objective. Bioplasm is not alive, but under the influence of Life — Divine Life — it begins to perform certain conduct, and for a specific purpose — for the production of a certain form. It is Life that does the work, while matter is the material out of which the form is made. Drummond further observes:

"To understand unmistakably that it is really the Potter who does the work, let us follow for a moment a description of the process by a trained eye-witness. The observer is Professor Thomas H. Huxley. Through the tube of his microscope he is watching the development, out of a speck of protoplasm, of one of the commonest animals: 'Strange possibilities; says he, 'lie dormant in that semi-fluid globule.'

"Let a moderate supply of warmth reach its watery cradle, and the plastic matter undergoes changes so rapidly, and yet so steady and purpose-like in their succession, that one can only compare them to those operated by a skilled modeler upon a formless lump of clay.

"As with an invisible trowel, the mass is divided and subdivided into smaller and smaller portion, until it is reduced to an aggregation of granules not too large to build withal the finest fabrics of the nascent organism. And then, it is as though a delicate finger traced out the line to be occupied by the spinal column, and molded the contour of the body; pinching up the head at one end, the tail at the other, and fashioning flank and limb into due proportions in so artistic a way, that, after watching the process hour by hour, one is almost involuntarily possessed by the notion, that some more subtle aid to vision than an achromatic would show the hidden artist, with his plan before him, striving with skillful manipulation to perfect the work."

Out of this speck of colorless protoplasm, the Hidden Artist begins the construction of a form of some kind — it may be plant or animal; it may be an oak or an ox; or a monkey or a man. What determines which it shall be? Drummond thinks that the kind of form depends upon the kind of potter. He remarks:

"And as there is only one clay, and yet all these curious forms are developed out of it, it follows necessarily that the difference lies in the potters. In Nature one potter is set apart to make each (kind of form). One artist makes all the dogs, another makes all the birds, a third makes all the men. Moreover, each artist confines himself exclusively to working out his own plan. He appears to have his own plan somewhat stamped upon himself, and his work is rigidly to reproduce himself."

The Professor is much mistaken in his observations. The kind of form does not depend upon the kind of potter; nor does "one artist make all the dogs, another make all the birds, and a third make all the men." There is one potter — The Great Potter; and He makes each and every kind of form. In conformity with the law, "each after their kind," the form is constructed by The Great Potter that shall resemble the form of the parents.

# Chapter No. 10
# When Man Begins to Live

In a minute speck of colorless colloid, in the uterus of the female, with "an invisible trowel," the Hidden Artist, "with his plan before him," begins to construct the form of man. Close your eyes and draw a mental picture of this marvelous, unexplainable phenomenon. Now watch closely, for if man is alive, or if he is Life, here and now is where and when that fact must be discovered and determined, or else the problem must always remain a mystery.

So far, this tiny speck of colorless colloid has shown no signs of life or of being alive. But watch the change take place. Doctor J. H. Kellogg observes:

"There is nothing more interesting in all the realm of science, than to watch with the microscope the operations of protoplasm. Let us study this wonderful phenomenon for a few minutes. Now we are rewarded by seeing just what we are in search of, curious little round masses so transparent as to be almost invisible. They are not very numerous, but scattered here and there about the field.

"Presently we perceive that some are changing their form. A moment ago the first one we inspected was as round as a watch crystal; now it has become elliptical in form. A few minutes later we look again, and it has stretched itself out in a long filament like an angle-worm. Presently it begins to draw itself up into a round mass again; and, before we can write it, it has assumed its original shape, but has changed its position.

"That is the way the little creature moves about. It makes itself into the shape of a worm, and then crawls just as a worm does, by making one end fast and drawing the rest of the body up. What does it move about for? Why may it not remain stationary?

"A few seconds ago it was as round as a full moon. Now there is a little pocket in one side. The pocket is growing deeper and deeper. What is the object of such curious procedure? The mystery is solved. There is a little speck of food which the little creature wishes to get, and so he has made a pocket to put is in. The queerest part is yet to come, so we must watch patiently a moment more. Now the mouth of the pocket is closing up. Evidently the little fellow is afraid he may lose the precious morsel, and so he is going to shut the pocket to prevent its escape. Now the opening is closed, and before we are aware of it, the pocket itself has disappeared, and there is the little particle inside.

"This seems a miraculous process, but it is the way these little creatures have of taking food. As we become better acquainted with proto-plasm, it does not seem so strange, after all, that it should be capable of making a plant, painting a flower, building a tree, or even of forming a man; and that is just what it does" (*Home Hand-Book*).

The tiny speck of colorless colloid, "so transparent as to be almost invisible," is commencing to move about, and this state is said to be "the beginning of a new life." From whence comes the "new life?" Does it come from the mother? Is the life of the mother also the life of the "new life?" Let us notice what Doctor Carver says:

"From the instant of the entrance of the spermatozoon into the ovum, marked and characteristic changes take place in its germinal part as well as in that of the male germinal part. These immediately begin conduct wholly distinct and different from that so far performed. The elements of the ovum approach the spermatozoon in what is known as the cone of attraction, as though welcoming its entrance and attempting to make safe and easy its path of movement.

"The germinal elements from being concentrated, separate into their particles, and the general cytoplasm of the ovum, as it is called, begins to be organized with relation to what are now called the male pro-nucleus and the female pro-nucleus, and as this arrangement occurs, the gametes or pronuclei travel toward each other.

"By the time they come near to each other, certain elements of each stand out separately, and coming nearer, these separate, individual particles merge and fuse, as it were, into each other, producing a clear field, in which nothing appears. Finally, after a period of seeming quiescence, granulation occurs at the point between the places occupied by the gametes when they disappeared (from sight).

"The granulated point is the beginning of the new person, and is called the Zygote or pre-embryo, the production of which completes the period of impregnation.

"It will be seen that where the gametes, floating in their fluids, differ from lymph corpuscles, for example, is at the entrance of the spermatozoon into the ovum. Up to that moment their life-history and conduct present nothing different from that of lymph corpuscles. The gametes have been acting in conformity with the energy animating the male and female organisms in which they were produced.

"Upon impregnation all is changed; they cease thus to act, and begin to act according to the law of a new energy, and in such manner as to produce a new organism, composed primarily of the material brought from the parents in the gametes. The temptation to enter the realm of speculation as to what this new energy is, that manifests itself at this juncture, will be repressed, for it has not yet been given to human beings to know.

"With regard to the animating force, it is sufficient, at this time, to say, that it is an intelligent energy, that fashions the organism, and maintains it to the instant of dissolution (death)" (*Psycho-Bio-Physiology,* page 194-5).

The life of the mother is not the life of the "new person." Nor is the life of the father the life of the "new person." For the male and the female gametes, floating in their fluids, exhibit no distinguishable difference from ordinary blood and lymph corpuscles, floating in their fluids. The male and the female gametes meet and fuse; they disappear from sight, leaving a "clear field" in which nothing is discernable. "Up to that moment," says Doctor Carver, "their life-history and conduct present nothing different from that of lymph corpuscles."

But after that, all is changed. The granules that come into view in the "clear field," begin to act according to the law of a "new energy, continues Doctor Carver, "and in such manner as to produce a new organism, composed primarily of the material brought from the parents in the gametes."

What about this "new energy?" What is it? Where was it before the gametes met, fused, and disappeared? Why did it appear afterwards? And if not there before, from whence came it?

The answer, apparently puzzling and complex, exceedingly simple, and devoid of confusion and mystery. To solve our problem we must discover the principle. What is that principle? It is, that God (Divine Life) is omnipotence, omniscience, and omnipresence. This we are taught, and this we believe. If we believe it, we have found ourselves; but if we believe it not, we are lost.

It is written that God is a Spirit; that the words that I speak unto you, they are spirit, and they are life. Spirit and Life are Interchangeable terms; they both mean the same thing. For it is the Spirit that quickeneth; the flesh profiteth nothing *(John 4:24; 6:63)*. The second man, that is the spirit that quickeneth, IS THE LORD FROM HEAVEN *(1 Corinthians 15:45)*.

If Life is Spirit, if Spirit is God, and if God omnipotence, omniscience, and omnipresence, then Life, the very Life that quickens the body when it is but an invisible speck in the female uterus, and builds that invisible speck into a 150-pound man, is omnipotence, omniscience, and omnipresence.

Life does not come from anywhere. It is here, there, and everywhere, now, ever, and always. In the "clear field" we had Divine Life cornered in a space so small that the microscope could not reveal it. We could see nothing, yet we know Divine Life is there, because we beheld evidence of a "new energy."

Would a more powerful aid to human vision reveal its presence? No. The clay cannot see the Potter. The receptive capacity of the human brain is limited. It can receive only so much intelligence as it can use, and no more. Less intelligence would be insufficient for the needs of the organism, and more would be superfluous.

Divine Life rigidly observes the Law of Economy. No animal is endowed beyond its needs, and none are given less than its needs require. Every living creature is endowed with capacity to receive from the Unlimited Source, sufficient intelligence to enable it to live in the environment in which it is usually placed. No more, and no less, is given to man. In order for man to have power to discover Divine Life, he would have to possess Divine Intelligence in its fullness; and in that event he would not be a man; he would not be a part of the animal kingdom. He would be Life in himself, instead of a lowly form of clay, through which Divine Life expresses itself. The "new energy" that fashions the organism and maintains it, from the moment of impregnation in the uterus of the female to the moment of death, is the Great Potter, the Hidden Artist, who wields the Mystic Trowel. On this point Pastor Russell makes the following remarks:

"The boldest and ablest scientists and evolutionists have attempted to show that man's life was not a gift from the Creator. Theoretically they have brought man and all the lower animals up, by evolution process, from a microscopic germ; yea, from protoplasm, which Professor Huxley called 'the physical basis of life;' and they fain would in some way ignore the Creator and Life-giver entirely; but, as a matter of fact, they have been unable to suggest any way that even protoplasm could get life from inert matter. To this extent, therefore, they are obliged to recognize a first great cause of life" (The *Atonement,* etc., page 398).

Here is the same error, as old as the race, and the one that Christ strove to correct. Life is not a gift from the

Creator; for Life IS the Builder, the Hidden Artist, the Creator, animating the lifeless form of clay. God is a Spirit, and it is the Spirit that quickeneth. The life that the organism appears to possess, is not life in itself, but is merely the movements of the material form as it is handled by the Great Potter. The body is merely animated by Divine Life. *In him we live, and move, and have our being*.

As to this Doctor Carver observes:

"Every animate substance in the entire realm of nature, gives unimpeachable proof that what we call living substance is nothing more than inanimate molecules, the relation of which is caused by a given energy to produce a new and different form of conduct, which conduct we call living. Substances so organized and energized we classify as being animated. In the abstract, the fact of animate substances consisting only in form and relationship of inanimate particles, formed and related according to the law of a given energy, only occurs to the student as being strange, because of the newness of the thought. and not because of a possibility of its inaccuracy."

Life, as we have said, is everywhere — in the matrix of the female as well as in the bowels of the earth, in the depth of the sea as well as in the vastness of the sky. Its manifestations become visible when it has material forms through which to express itself. But is cannot build these forms until there exist the conditions demanded by law. When and where these conditions do exist, the Spiritual World (The Father), and the Material World (The Mother), meet and unite — and the Great Union thus formed is God in the Ultimate and Absolute.

The apparent complexity and mystery are so because we fail to find the principle back of them. We cannot find the principle because we cannot find the Father. We are lost; and the Son of Man came to save that which is lost *(Matthew 18:11)*. But he was rejected because a material world could not comprehend his words of Spirit and of Truth *(John 6:63)*.

Lost men live in the material world, and live not, for the material does not live. Men who find the Father live in the Spiritual World, and know that the Father alone hath life in Himself. It was to the lost men that Christ spoke these words:

You are from beneath (from the dust); I am from above (spirit); ye are of this world (dust); I am not of this world (dust) *(John 8:23)*.

Christ shut his eyes to the material world, and so found the Father. Other men will find the Father only when they do likewise. When men cast off the teaching that worships the shadow, and lift the veil that hides the light, they will find Truth; and then complexity and mystery will yield to unity and simplicity.

Life, Divine Life, God the Father, is present everywhere and always. But before we can perceive this majestic presence, Life must clothe itself with a material form. The moment the ovum is impregnated by the spermatozoon of the male, the condition suitable for the visible manifestation of Life is supplied; and Life lays hold of the ovum at this instant, and the gametes "begin to act according to the law of a new energy, and in such manner as to produce a new organism."

The individual existence of the "new person" begins at this moment; and from now on the growth of the "new person" is accomplished by the systematic addition of new material to the tiny speck of colorless colloid, under the direct influence of the "new energy."

But the "new energy" does not grow. "For it is unthinkable," says Doctor Carver, "to conceive that Life can grow." It is the "new person" that grows, and the growth results from "the relation of elements," continued Doctor

Carver, "under the domination of a given energy, and the whole is (animated) and individualized by that energy."

Since Life is, and does not and cannot grow, then the Life that animates the "new person" from his earliest existence is the same Life that continues to express itself through the form of the "new person," from the first to the last, from the instant the ovum is impregnated to the instant of death. The reason that Life appears to express itself more fully as the form grows, is because the form, becoming more complete day by day, is capable of more complete expression of the force that animates it.

Thus we observe that man is not alive. His body is never more than inert matter. "It is the spirit that quickeneth, the body profiteth nothing," says Christ *(John 6:63)*. As the body moves under the quickening force of Life, we are deceived, we see and see not, and we think the body is alive. The fact is that it is only quickened by the spirit — and the entire teaching of Christ was directed to the task of trying to impress that truth on the mind of man. The reader should remember well the things just related. For he must come to a day when he will be required to "lay down his life;" and he will then wonder whether his "soul" is destined for "heaven" or "hell."

Consider the gross falsity inherent in a theology that teaches that man has a "soul" which takes a long "flight" after death, and lands in either "heaven" or "hell," depending on that man's conduct during his lifetime.

There is no such thing as "soul" as that term is generally understood. Soul is individualized Spirit or Divine Life. The body is composed of Matter that is animated by Divine Life. That is all man is. Death is a term signifying the separation of Divine Life from Matter. As Divine Life, when its presence was first detected in the impregnated ovum, came from nowhere, being everywhere, being omnipresence, why shall we believe that it must take a long journey after death?

The Life that animates the impregnated ovum, is the same Life that leaves the body at death, and it has remained unchanged from the first to the last. When it leaves the body, — Then shall the dust return to the earth as it was; and the spirit shall return unto God who gave it *(Ecclesiastes 12:7)*.

When Divine Life leaves the body, it returns to the place it came from.

# Chapter No. 11
# Relation Of Man To Life

In the uterus of the female, from particles of matter so minute that nothing but a "clear field" is visible under the microscope, Divine Life begins to build the human form. The process from this moment until death is, in its broadest sense, one of construction and destruction.

The physical body is built of particles extracted from air, water, soil, and sunshine. With this material, Divine Life constructs a definite form after a definite pattern. The pattern is that impressed upon the colorless colloid by inheritance. As rapidly as material is built into the body, it is used up, worn out, broken down, and cast off; and with the same regularity, new parts out of new material are rebuilt into their places.

By the aid of the microscope, we can follow the new building material down in the body, before birth and after birth, in the child or in the adult, until it finally passes from the field of vision, because of the minuteness of the divisions which it undergoes. Before it passes out of sight, we could perceive no change of the new built material into any particle that resembled a cell or the molecule of a cell. After it passes out of sight nothing is known of the process that occurs.

The process of construction and destruction is performed in the interstitial spaces of the body — that is to say, in the inter-spaces between the cells. We should remember that cells are composed of hundreds of molecules, that molecules are composed of hundreds of atoms, that atoms are composed of hundreds of ions, and so on — and that atoms are the smallest particles that are large enough to be seen with the microscope. Yet, in this invisible realm within the body, between the invisible particles of which the body is composed, Divine Life performs all function of the body — not only that of construction and destruction of the cells, molecules, atoms, etc., but of every function, whatever it may be. How these functions are performed, man will never know, and physiology will remain a mystery.

We have seen that the body itself, from the first, does nothing of itself. Behind it, over it, or shall we say within it, is and remains from the first to the last, the Hidden Artist — the force we call Divine Life, for the want of better terminology.

In the "clear field, in which nothing appears, finally, after a period of seeming quiescence, granulation occurs at a point between the places occupied by the gametes when they disappeared. The granulation point is the beginning of the new person."

As the Hidden Artist begins the work of arranging colorless colloids into definite form, "a new and different form of conduct, which conduct we call living," becomes plainly evident. This "new and different form of conduct" did not arise in, nor come from, the colorless colloid; because we know from every day experience that if the Hidden Artist should withdraw his mysterious and elusive presence, the signs of life — the "new and different form of conduct" — would immediately vanish.

When the Hidden Artist begins, in the female uterus, the work of weaving colorless colloid into definite form, the signs of life for the first time are visible. Life is not part of the colorless colloid, for its presence cannot be detected until at a certain time, and then we can tell that the Hidden Artist has arrived, only because of the peculiar and definite conduct exhibited by the colorless colloid.

It is the operation of the Hidden Artist upon and within the material form, that makes men believe they are alive. That is all there is of life in man, from beginning to end, from the time the speck of colorless colloid begins to move, until the day when the Hidden Artist withdraws from the form, and the state called death ensues.

Divine Life is the invisible force that moves; matter is the visible form that is moved. Seeing the effect of the operation of Divine Life in and on matter, but not seeing Divine Life, and not understanding its presence, we think that matter, because it moves, is alive. We mistake the effect for the cause. Men make the same mistake in many, many ways. We see what appears to be the Sun revolving around the Earth, and once believed that this was a fact. He now knows that it is only an illusion. It is the appearance that deceives the sense of man, and leads him to believe that he is Life.

The ray of light passes invisibly through space, and is seen only when it falls on an object. Divine Life passes invisibly through all space, and permeates and penetrates all things, down into the deepest recesses of the earth; but only when it operates through organized forms, does its majestic presence become known. It is the effect that we see, for the Divine Life is not visible on the material plane. No man hath seen God (Divine Life) at any time *(John 1:18)*. But the presence of the Hidden Artist is known through its works.

Without the form of man as the instrument through which to work, Divine Life could not express itself in its highest state, and the green globe on which we live would have remained a vast wilderness of forests and jungles. Without Divine Life to construct his body and animate it, man could not have come into existence, much less do the things which he appears to do, and which he thinks he does of himself. As a man thinketh in his heart, so he is. How can we ever change the thought that man is Life? How can we make him understand that it is the spirit that quickeneth, while the flesh profiteth nothing?

Man is not alive. He has no more to do with the work which he thinks he performs, than has the violin with the marvelous melodies drawn from its depths by the bow of the artist.

Man is only an instrument. So is the violin. Back of the violin is the living artist. He constructs the violin for a specific purpose. Could the violin perform that purpose without the artist? Without the artist, the violin could not have come into existence. After coming into existence, it could do nothing but for the artist. It would be a dead, inert wood and glue and strings. So also the artist, without the violin, would be unable to express to the world, the melodious music of the storm, the rhythmic gurgle of the cataract, the laughter of children, the sweet strains of the mocking bird — the wonderful harmonies surging through his soul.

It is impossible, by the use of material illustrations, to paint an accurate picture of the relation of the material to the immaterial, of the physical to the spiritual, of the instrument to the worker, of the violin to the artist, of the body to its Divine Operator and Performer.

The body, like the violin, had nothing to do with its formation, organization, and construction. The body is only the clay in the hands of the Potter. Behind it is the Hidden Artist, which we call Divine Life — that great mystery which none can know, and which ever remains invisible. Life is a force. The fact of its unexplainable mystery does not detract from its reality. Nor is the reality a mere mental conception; it is the substantial force called Life. No man has seen. it; no man will ever see it. We behold only its manifestation. It is the Hidden Artist that is responsible for all we know, and see, and do.

While the body is eternally changing, the Hidden Artist remains the same. From the instant the ovum is impregnated to the instant of death, the Hidden Artist, the Divine Life, remains unchanged. As the infant grows, and finally comes to maturity it appears that Life grows, that the body expresses Life to greater degree. And the body does express Life to greater degree; but this is so only because, as the body grows, it becomes more capable of greater expression. Life does not grow. It is the body that grows.

# Chapter No. 12
# Man is Not Life

Divine Life is God and God is Divine Life. Man lives because Divine Life flows through his body. Yet Divine Life is no more confined in the body it quickens, than substance is confined in its shadow. "Life is imminent in such structures," says Doctor Carver, "but not inherent in them."

If Life were inherent in the structure, it would be part of the structure. But it is no more part of the structure, than is the Sun part of its reflection upon the face of the earth. If the earth were not, there would be no reflection of the Sun's rays from it; but that would not affect nor efface the Sun.

A man begins his individual existence the moment that the minute gametes, composing his tiny organism, are separated into their consisting particles, and are re-arranged and related to constitute a separate entity. This makes it clear that animal forms are not alive, but are just animated particles of matter, constructed by Life into a definite form, which, without the animating force of Life, would be nothing more than inert matter (Carver).

Man is not Life. Man is not even alive. He is but a material instrument through which Life operates, and Life continues such operation so long as the instrument complies and conforms in every detail with the law. A man's feeling that he is Life, or that he is alive, instead of being the instrument through which Life expresses itself, arises from appearance only. He thinks he is Life, when in fact he is merely an organized form of matter, so constructed that Life can operate through his body.

Should we be surprised at this last statement? We observe force operating through matter on all sides of us, and think it a very ordinary occurrence. Contemplate the things that are accomplished by the operation of electricity through a copper wire. It is not the wire that does the work. We speak of such a wire as being "alive." But if we cut off the current flowing thru it, instead of a "live wire" we have a "dead wire," a wire that can do nothing; and yet the wire itself, to all appearances, has undergone no visible change.

We see a man performing work, and we say that he is alive. He is alive only in the same sense that the copper wire is alive. The reason why man can perform more complicated work than a wire can is because man is a more complicated structure than a wire is, and because the force flowing through his form is the highest degree of force known. It is a force of infinite intelligence, which not only operates through matter, but which constructs matter into a multitude of forms in order to perform a multitudinous variety of work.

Regardless of how much life a man appears to possess, or how much he seems to be alive, he becomes just as dead as the wire the moment the flow of Life through his form is cut off. The speeding runner, exhibiting in his body the Divine Life throbbing at its highest rate, suddenly has his heart pierced with the deadly rifle ball, and his form immediately sinks into an immovable heap upon the ground, to rise no more by virtue of the power which it appeared before to possess.

What has happened? The flow of Life through the body has been cut off. The form of clay no longer complies with the requirements of the law governing animated bodies, and so Divine Life departs there from, showing that the body is just animated particles of matter which, without the animating force of Life, become nothing more than an inert mass of clay. Thus we observe that a man is no more alive than is a copper wire. Man makes copper wire to convey electrical force for the purpose of performing certain kinds of work.

The Creator make man in order that He may express Himself through man, and operate through man for the purpose of performing work on the visible plane that could not otherwise be performed.

This knowledge brings us squarely face to face with the fact, that it is literally true, that in Him we live, and move, and have our being, as the poets have unconsciously said *(Acts 17:28)*. We often wonder whether the one who uttered these words, realized how true they are. And yet how faintly a few of us comprehend the great truth here, because false conceptions and miss-education as to Divine Life have closed our eyes and perverted our understanding, so that seeing, we see not, and hearing, we hear not *(Mark 8:18)*.

The Master dug down and found the spiritual man. He was not deluded by the deception of sight. He knew what Life is, and endeavored to convey the information to a lost world. He declared that he knew the Father, because He lived by the Father. But the religious world rejected His teachings, just as it did that of the Seers and the Prophets who preceded Him and who come after Him. Sixteen hundred years after Christ, Bruno is burned by a fanatical priesthood for teaching the doctrine which Christ taught, and which is taught us by every living thing on the face of the earth.

The sixth chapter of John clearly explains the whole thing. But since the belief in material things now, as then, closes the eyes, stops the ears, and shuts up the understanding *(Matthew 13:13-17),* few men of this age can read that chapter and get any more out of it, than did the multitude get out of the spoken words of Jesus.

Jesus declared that He lived by the Father *(John 6:57)*. There is nothing strange or marvelous about that. Had He said that He did not live by the Father, and then indeed would we know that He was in error. Every man lives by the One Common Father Of All, without which nothing is or can be. Man does not live by his material father, for his material father, having no life in himself, has none to give. Every man lives by the Father, which is the Spiritual Father, the Divine Life. Man is the image of the Father, not in flesh but in spirit. God is a Spirit. It is the Father alone that hath "Life in Himself."

This is the bread (Divine Life) which came down from heaven. I do not mean the (material) bread that your fathers ate, and are dead; for he that eightieth of this bread (Divine Life) shall live forever *(John 6:58)*.

What bread did He refer to? The bread which came down from heaven. What kind of bread was it that came down from heaven? The Breath Of Life *(Genesis 2:7)* the spiritual body; the Lord from heaven *(1 Corinthians 15:44-47)*. It is the "living soul" which came down from heaven; for the material form is of the earth, earthy.

This statement was too much, even for the disciples. They murmured at such astonishing declarations; they were steeped in materialism; they thought only in terms of materialism; consequently, it was very logical that they should fail to grasp the spiritual aspect of the situation. The Master tried to clear away the fog with this clean-cut statement:

It is the spirit that quickened); the flesh profiteth nothing; the words that I speak to you, they are spirit, and they are life *(John 6:63)*.

There is no room for doubt here, for this plain language puts all doubt at rest for once and for all. The flesh is not Life; in fact, it is not even alive, for it profits nothing because it is quickened by the spirit — by the "bread which came down from heaven." Jesus is not talking about the flesh, for he says, *THE WORDS THAT I SPEAK TO YOU, THEY ARE SPIRIT, AND THEY ARE LIFE*. He was talking about the spirit, about life — Divine Life, that great, majestic, marvelous, elusive force which men in every age have sought to know, and which they refuse to understand when explained to them.

From this time on many of his disciples went back and walked no more with him *(John 6:66)*. They could not understand. It did not fit and fill the space in their heart. They were looking for temporal greatness. Divine Life meant nothing to them.

Why do ye not understand my speech? even because ye cannot hear my word. Because I tell you the truth, ye believe me not. Which of you convinceth me of sin? And if I say the truth, why do ye not believe me *(John 8:43, 45, 46)*.

Today, almost twenty long centuries since the message of Spirit and of Life failed to dent the ivory domes of the materialists, men believe that Life is nothing more than the reaction of a chemical formula; the stinking gas rising from the decomposition of matter. They still believe that Life is a thing that originated in the salty sea, and that man, by ages of struggle, succeeded in wresting from Nature, and did not receive from the Creator, all the various parts and members of his marvelous body, which body he thinks is alive.

# Chapter No. 13
## Man Does Nothing of Himself

If man could be made to understand that it is the Spirit that quickeneth, and that the flesh profiteth nothing, such knowledge would open up to him more startling truths than have been discovered in all the ages past. It is written:

Without me ye can do nothing. The Father that dwelleth in me, he doeth the works *(John14:10)*. For it is God which worketh in you both to will and to do His good pleasure *(Philippians 2:13)*.

The Christian world thinks these pretty phrases. But do men believe in them? The so-called Christian shows by his conduct that he has less faith in them, than he has in the declaration —

*"In Him we live, and move, and have our being."*

To prove that man can do nothing of himself, we need only consider the marvelous apparatus by which man is made acquainted with his surroundings — the special senses. For the purpose at hand, a consideration of the eye, the organ of sight, is sufficient, since the same philosophy is employed in the explanation of each organ of sensation.

Does the eye see? Can the open eye of a dead man see? If the eye is possessed in itself of the power of sight, then the open eye of a dead man could see equally as well as the eye of a living man. For what is lacking in death that is not lacking in life?

But some will argue that the power of sight resides in the optic nerve and the brain. Granting this to be true, then the eye of the dead man should be able to see as well as the eye of the living man, so long as the connection between the eye, the optic nerve, and the brain remains intact. For if the power of sight arises in and comes from the brain, out through the optic nerve to the eye, why should so small a change as the absence of Life interfere with the operation of the power of sight?

If the power of sight resides in the brains, then the absence of Life would be incapable of restricting or destroying that power. But since the absence of Life totally destroys the power or sense of sight, together with all the other functions of the body, we know that the sense of sight, instead of residing in the brain, arises as the direct effect of the operation of Life through the brain, and through the optic nerve, to the eye.

The eye is but lenses through which light vibrations enter from the outer world. These vibrations reach the optic nerve, through the vibrations of the vitreous body of the eyeball, and are transmitted over the optic nerve to the brain. In the brain Divine Life transforms into intelligence, the sensation produced by the material world coming in contact with Divine Life through this particular and specifically constructed channel. The result is what we call sight, which in fact is merely a mental state; for the brain cannot see any more than the eye can see. However, we do not desire to leave the impression that all is mind and mind is all. The mind would be as blank as the empty sky, if no visible objects existed to call the mind into activity.

The eye of itself has no more capacity to see than has a glass-eye lying in a jewelry store. For the eye is only matter, composed of material that comes from the dust of the ground, and is constructed by Life into its unique and particular form. The same remarks apply with equal force to the optic nerve, the brain, and each and every other part of the body.

The material body, let us repeat, is simply an instrument, as we are so often told in the Scriptures, by means of which Life (Spirit) produces certain changes and performs certain functions on the Visible Plane. Hence, when Life is withdrawn from the body, the body is without sensation, for the body has no sensation in itself. Therefore, we know that all sensation, which man erroneously believes comes from his body, actually comes from the operation of Life in and through his body.

The body, being nothing more than the material instrument that furnishes Life an avenue through which to operate on the Visible Plane, upon the departure of Life from the body, which event is called death; the material world can no longer be sensated by the body, because the power of sensation resides not in the body, but in Divine Life.

The Great Teacher was not deceived by appearances; for He lived by faith and not by sight. Being guided by the teaching of the great Moses, who believed in a material man and a spiritual man, Jesus dug down beneath the material surface and found the spiritual man — *THE WAY, THE TRUTH, AND THE LIFE (John 14:6).*

By virtue of this discovery, He knew that He and the Father were one and inseparable, for He knew that His Life was but an expression the Great Spirit in and through his material form. He tried to teach this great truth to men, but because of their false belief in relation to Life, they could not understand Him.

He told them:

"I and my Father are one. The Father is in me, and I in Him *(John 11:30-38)*. The words that I speak unto you, I speak not of myself; but the Father that dwelleth in me, He doeth the works" *(John 14:10)*.

Likewise, every man and the Father are one. The Father is in every man, and every man is in the Father. The words that appear to speak, they speak not of themselves; but the Father that dwelleth in them, He it is that doeth the works. Otherwise, how could it be that God is ALL IN ALL? and that in Him we live, and move, and have our being?

# Chapter No. 14
# Influence of Training and Tradition

We have no especial desire to pick a quarrel with the preachers. They are but the human product of their material environment. To this extent they are not liable for the gross ignorance exhibited in the field of their labor. As a man thinketh in his heart, so is he. And men's thoughts are the product of their surroundings, the belief of their ancestors, the age in which they live, the education they receive, the errors they are compelled to accept, the traditions of their land, the customs of their country, the doctrines of their day.

Few men of the past have had the strength and courage to rise above this ruling plane, take the molten calf made for them by their tutors, burn it in the fire, and grind it to powder, and strew it upon the water. For experience discloses that to do so is dangerous. Bloodshed and persecution, the hemlock and the rack, the stake and the cross, have always awaited those who dared question the settled opinions of the times.

Men are securely held in line by a carefully planned system of miss-education. The human mind must not be permitted to develop, expand, and burst asunder the venerable doctrines and traditions of the past. Each succeeding generation must be kept in the beaten path of stupidity and superstition. To this end, society sets apart the years of the young, when the mind is tender, plastic, and undeveloped, for instructing them in the absurd lore and twaddle of past ages, thus effectively moulding their mind to fit the false forms of yesterday, instead of developing it to create new and better forms for the morrow.

Few will admit it, but it is a fact nevertheless, that the influence of tradition and the educational systems of society, hold men today in bondage as firm and as absolute, as that which enslaved the children of Israel under the galling yoke of the Egyptian Pharaohs. And this blasting influence the minister of the gospel cannot escape.

Every Sunday at church, in every corner of Christendom, the dignified doctor of divinity, a man generally respected and reverenced by his flock for his supposed possession of the Truth that makes men free, with much solemnity rises up from his seat, folds his arms across his manly chest, closes his eyes, bows his gray head, and fervently invokes the personal God of Christianity to hear him, and to bless, protect, aid, and assist all those "dear ones" within the sound of the word apparently spoken by his material lips.

Can the Clay speak to the Potter? Can the Flesh, which never lived, commune with the Spirit, which alone is Life? Does matter of, and from itself, have the capacity of thought, action, speech, etc.? What is meant by "In Him we live, and move, and have our being?" Also it is written:

*"For it is not ye that speak, but the Spirit of your Father which speaketh in you (Matthew10:20)."*

It is said that we are progressing in matters of religion as well as in other pursuits; but we still persist in believing that men pray, act, talk, think, move, and live, when it is clearly taught that the Spirit of the Lord speaks through us, and that His words are in our tongue. *(2 Samuel 23:2).*

How can prejudiced, biased, bigoted people be made to understand, that if Life, call it Soul, Spirit, God, or what you will, did not animate the material form of their ministers, did not move their lips of dust, did not speak, as it were, from their material mouth, the very words that men appear to utter, in praising their personal God, could never form, nor sound, nor leave their material lips. Being so ignorant of material existence, how utterly ignorant such men must be of spiritual existence.

# Chapter No. 15
## Ancient Worship Rules Today

The modern custom of worship, like the modern practice of medicine, is the child of ancient idolatry — of bloody animal and human sacrifice. Men have always craved some material form of worship. They have been idolaters from the dawn of human history, and have worshipped various objects, ranging from deadly reptiles to golden calves, from Moloch, the "fire god," to sacred bulls *(Exodus 32:4)*.

Professor N. N. Riddell observes:

"The tendency to worship the supernatural is an innate attribute of human nature. It is said that there has never been discovered a race or tribe of people but that had some form of worship. The objects of their worship have been as variable as human invention, fancy, and fear could conceive of — man has worshipped almost everything in nature, from the pebble that he crushes beneath his feet to the sun that lights the universe" *(Human Nature Explained,* page 281).

Some races have worshipped the sun, moon, and stars. Others have deified animals, as the Egyptians, who worshipped the sacred bull Apis. Of the wise King Solomon, it is written:

"Then did Solomon build an high place for Chemo's, the abomination of Moab, in the hill that is before Jerusalem, and for Motech, the abomination of the children of Amman. And likewise did he for all his strange wives, which burnt incense and sacrificed unto their gods *(1 Kings 11:7, 8)."*

Again we read:

"And they have built the high places of Tophet, which is

in the valley of the son of Hinnom, to burn their sons and their daughters in the fire. And they built the high places of Baal, which are in the valley of the son of Hinnom, to cause their sons and their daughters to pass through the fire unto Moloch" *(Jeremiah 7:31, 32, 35).*

And again we read:

"And they served their idols; which were a snare unto them. Yea, they sacrificed their sons and their daughters unto devils. And shed innocent blood, even the blood of their sons and of their daughters, whom they sacrificed unto the idols of Canaan: and the land was polluted with blood *(Psalm 106:36-38)."*

Here we find a written account of the "chosen people of God," erecting iron gods, building roaring fires in them, then casting their children into this red-hot furnace to be consumed by its furious flames. And no doubt their God looked on, and was pleased, and approved the procedure.

However, it may have grieved some of the people in their heart, to indulge in this sort of "god worship." Some must have shed tears to see their children offered in such bloody sacrifice. Yet they believed in it, because they were educated into that faith; and the education was prescribed by rulers steeped in prejudice, superstition, egotism, selfishness, and murder.

These people were the slaves of their merciless rulers and leaders. They were kept in ignorance in order that they might not discover truth. And when the Great Teacher showed them the way, the truth, and the life *(John 14:6),* the rulers knew that the end of their day was near, unless they promptly took some drastic action.

The rank and file of this age fail to realize how completely they are in bondage. Many will not believe it when so informed. Others, being slaves of their deceivers, join with the selfish "powers that be," in the persecution of them who strive to show that the hand of the tyrant is at man's throat today, just as surely as in the past. The iron hand of medical tyranny, for instance, is slowly closing on the throat of civilization. As an enemy of man, it will soon rival the Inquisition established by Pope Gregory IX in, 1235.

When physicians take the filthy pus, drawn from the belly of a sick calf, and deliberately inject it into the pure bloodstream of your child, and unqualifiedly declare to you, with a look of assurance on their faces, that this procedure will protect your child from disease, then by lectures, by press propaganda, by the persecution of all who oppose it, and by every other conceivable means, instill into your mind such education as keeps you in total ignorance of the truth, and leads you to believe in and submit to that idolatrous practice of poisoning, you can sum it all up by saying, you are also shedding innocent blood, even the blood of your children, and are sacrificing to idols that are a snare to you, just as surely as did people in the days of King Solomon.

And you ask, If that statement be true, why does the law allow it? The law allows it because the lying scoundrels, who do these dastardly deeds for gold, have paid lobbyists to procure legislation to this very end.

Have you forgotten that it was the love of gold, and not the love of truth, that prompted Demetrius, the silversmith, to call the craftsmen together, and show them that the teaching of the doctrine of Christ in their land, not only put their trade in danger "to be set at naught," — "but also that the temple of the great goddess Diana should be despised, and her magnificence should be destroyed, whom all Asia and the world worshipeth" *(Acts 19:24-27)*.

The speech of Demetrius, the maker of idols for an idolatrous people, had the desired effect, and the disciples of Christ were glad to get out of that country with their lives. Today innocent men and women are being sent to prison because they oppose vaccination and inoculation. Show us the progress and the freedom of which we boast. Is not our boast but an empty sound that dins our ears and deceives our understanding?

The God of the Israelites was not a spiritual God, but a man-invented Jehovah of love, repentance, anger, wrath, vengeance, murder, and all the other qualities of human weakness and changeableness *(Genesis 6 and 7; Exodus 32).* Let us see — And they heard the voice of God walking in the garden in the cool of the day *(Genesis 3:8).* And God said, Behold, the man is become one of us, to know good and evil *(Genesis 3:22).* In addition to talking many times, this God was human enough to repent that he had made man *(Genesis 6:6);* and to smell the sweet savor of the sacrifice *(Genesis 8:21)* and when Moses pleaded with Him that His wrath may not wax hot against the people, "the Lord repented of the evil which he thought to do unto his people" *(Exodus 32:10-14).*

God could write, and did write on two tables, and gave them to Moses; and Moses took them and started back to camp, but lost his temper and cast the tables out of his hands, breaking them beneath the mount, when he saw that while he was gone to talk with God, the people had made a golden calf and were worshiping the same as "thy gods which brought thee up out of the land of Egypt" *(Exodus 32:4-15-19).*

This God had been a hunter, for he set his bow in the clouds *(Genesis 9:13).* He also came down to earth to inspect the city and the tower, which the children of men builded *(Genesis 11:5).* And he had quite a discussion with Moses, and upon the entreaty of Moses to see his glory, Moses was permitted to see his "back parts" *(Exodus 33:13-18-23).*

The reason given for certain laws of cleanliness around the desert camps of the Hebrews, was that God walked the ways between the tents at night, and might soil his feet

(Wood). God also was a God of blood and war, as well as a God of all love. In the 10th Chapter of Joshua we learn that God fought for Israel (14), and that Joshua smote all the country of the hills, and of the south, and of the vale, and of the springs, and all their kings: he left none remaining, but utterly destroyed all that breathed, as God commanded (40).

The Christian's Bible states that his God is a Spirit *(John 4:24)*. How does this God differ from the God of the Israelites? Materialists must have something to worship that is more material than Spirit. So the Spirit has been worked over to conform to the material God of the Israelites, and held to be ALL LOVE, yet possessing the material qualities that make men devils, and the world a hell. Very wisely, this God was safely placed in a mysterious nowhere of eternal peace, plenty, and happiness, located millions of miles "above" the earth, in the ethereal regions of blue, where He sits on the Golden Throne, waving His magic scepter of omnipotent power, with the Saints doing His bidding, while angels play dulcet strains on golden harps. To this far off, unknown shore, from which no man returneth, the "good" go after death, and abide forever with the white-winged angels, while the unfortunate "bad" take the opposite route, which lands them in the sizzling pit of eternal fire and brimstone.

This is the best pen picture that we are capable of drawing, with our inadequate mode of language expression, of the "personal God Worship," conceived in the minds of the ancients, passed down from generation to generation, modified from time to time to comply with changing conditions and bring it up-to-date, believed in by the son because the father and grandfather believed in it, and regarded, yea, reverend today by millions of unthinking people, as being the truth without mistake.

We do not have to go far back in history until we come to a time and place, when the "inspired" leaders of the religious world passed their precious time in ordering conscientious and courageous heretics burned at the stake, and in discoursing upon the conditions of heaven and hell, and having the streets of heaven paved with glittering gold, the walls adorned with priceless jewels, and the gates made of pearls. Because these earthly treasures meant so much to these men here, they must have plenty of them in their eternal home above, or else peace, plenty, and happiness could not reign there.

It were well for their personal God, that the pagan idolater and mentally enslaved worshipper have taken care to place Him at such a safe distance from their baneful influence. For a closer association with these flesh-eating, money-grabbing, Mammon-loving, world-lusting folks would strain to the bursting point, even the unlimited love of a personal God.

The prime motive back of all manner of worship, is the stupid thought of appeasing the "wrath of an angry God," that is said to be all love. Why should God be angry? The sinner prays for forgiveness and mercy, and asks to be "saved." Saved from what? Saved from his sin? or saved in his sin? Does the sinner expect his sin to be forgiven, while he remains a slave to the sin? Why not forsake the sin, and thus make unnecessary the saving process that is costing the people so much wealth and the preachers so much worry? This money and man-power might then be turned into beneficial pursuits.

If this personal God were a God of anger, wrath, and murder, and still a Just God, as it is taught from the pulpit, why should law-abiding Christians fear Him? Fear does not affect nor chill the heart of the innocent. If His children obey His mandates, why should a Just God be angry? Law breakers are the only ones who have cause to fear the weight and wrath of their rulers.

It has been well said that "A guilty conscience makes cowards of us all." A guilty conscience needs no accuser. It was a guilty conscience that made the first man run away and hide in the depth of the forest; and it is a guilty conscience that makes modern man implore forgiveness and mercy. The materialist, who prays loudest and longest, feels that he is guiltiest. Are laws to be disobeyed at pleasure, and the prescribed penalty set aside by a prayer? Religion says, yes.

# Chapter No. 16
# In Spirit and in Truth

According to John, Christ gave to the world the following remarkable revelation of the Divine Life that men call God, together with specific directions how to serve or worship the Divine Life. He said:

But the hour cometh, and now is, when the true worshippers shall worship the Father (Divine Life) in Spirit and in Truth. God is a Spirit (Divine Life): and they that worship Him must worship Him in Spirit and in Truth *(John 4:23, 24)*.

It requires no university education to interpret the meaning of that plain and pointed statement. God is not a material being; and He cannot be worshipped in material form. He MUST be worshipped in Spirit and in Truth. The language of Spirit (Divine Life) must be spiritual (obedience). There is no alternative; it can be performed in no other way.

How shall we worship the Master in Spirit and in Truth? Let us see. The first law laid down had to do with man's conduct as to the care of his body. He was commanded not to maltreat it, and positively informed that if he committed crimes against his body, the penalty would be death *(Genesis 2:16, 17)*. More than four thousand years later, a certain lawyer, apparently having forgotten this law, asked:

Master, which is the great commandment in the law *(Matthew 22:36)?*

And the answer is:

Thou shalt love the Lord thy God with all thy heart, and with all thy soul, and with all thy mind. This is the first and great commandment. And the second is like unto it, Thou shalt love thy neighbor as thyself. On these two commandments hang all the law and the prophets *(Matthew 22:37, 38, 39, 40)*.

The location also of the kingdom of God is pointed out: The kingdom of God cometh not with observation; for, behold, the kingdom of God is within you *(Luke 17:20, 21)*.

And the Christian is further informed:

Know ye not that ye are the temple of God, and that the Spirit of God dwelled in you? If any man defile the temple of God, him shall God destroy: for the temple of God is holy, which temple ye are *(I Corinthians 3:16, 17). For ye are the temple of the living God (1 Corinthians 6:16)*.

The body of man is of the earth, earthy, and it is called the natural body. The force that animates the earthy body is the "Breath of Life," which is called the spiritual body, the second man, the Lord from heaven *(1 Corinthians 15:44-47)*. Then what men by habit call their "life," is nothing more nor less than the God-Spirit-Soul-Breath Of Life flowing through their material form, which has been explained. The material form of man, therefore, is the Temple of the Living God (Divine Life). This Temple is what we implore a "personal God" to save. For it is useless to ask Him to save our life, but is the Spirit (Divine Life), the great I AM, flowing through our material frame.

While praying God to save His temple, which Temple our body is, we heap upon that Temple every abuse and insult that can be conceived in the heart of man, every imagination of the thoughts of which is only evil continually *(Genesis 6:5)*.

If we would find the highest, the fullest, and the richest life that we can ever hope to know, we must forsake the false teaching that separates human life from Divine Life. There is only one Life and that is The Divine Life which we feel throbbing and vibrating through our material form

To communicate with the Divine Life, our prayers must be directed inward. To communicate with the Great Soul, it must be done through our Soul; for it is through our Soul only that we can reach the Great Soul, that is the only channel of communication between the Potter and the Clay — the Maker and the Made.

The Creator did not make man, and leave man no means by which to communicate with his Master. There is an avenue, which we shall later have occasion to observe more in particular, through which message may pass to and fro between man and his Master, between our Soul and the Great Soul. That avenue leads from the Mind inward, through the Soul to the "kingdom of God within." Should this seem strange, improbable, or impossible? Where should God be but within His kingdom?

It is hypocrisy to the last degree that educates men to worship the Divine Life, while giving no heed to the harmful habits which destroy the Temple in which Divine Life abides. It is a false theology that fails to teach men not to abuse their bodies, by a method of living that is based on erroneous ideas, and destructive beyond imagination.

Few men are hard-hearted enough to destroy the home of their meanest enemy; and no man could be persuaded to destroy the dwelling place of the neighbor he loved as he loves himself. And if we want God to believe that we love Him, we must make it our life-work, each day we live, to learn how to care for and preserve His Temple, then diligently live, each day of our life, what we thus learn.

So far, no man, not from the first, has worshipped God in Spirit and Truth by bestowing upon his body, the Temple of Divine Life, that scrupulous and conscientious care which men are commanded to give, in order to obey the law of their being.

By misuse and abuse of the genital organs alone, man falls far below the lowest beast of the field. Men gave themselves up to uncleanness through the lust of their own

hearts, to dishonor their own bodies between themselves.
Even their women did change the natural use into that which
is against Nature: And likewise also the men, leaving the
natural use of the woman, burned in their lust one toward
another *(Romans 1:24-27)*.

It seems as though Paul is speaking of this day and time,
for observe how prevalent today is the condition which he
mentions. Nineteen hundred years of Christianity seems to
have made little progress toward lifting man to a higher plane
of living. And if Christianity has failed in that respect,
wherein has it succeeded? One writer observes: "The
Christian nations are those that are shocked by one another's
atrocities."

Fornicators and adulterers, men have always been,
notwithstanding that he who committed fornication, sinneth
against his own body *(1 Corinthians 6:18);* and by sinning
against his body, man sinks into the lowest pit of vice, and
sins against the temple of the Living God, which temple God
has animated with His Spirit, thus giving it what we call life.

How shall we worship the Father in Spirit and in
Truth? Very simple: And when thou prayest, thou shalt not be
as the hypocrites are: for they love to pray standing in the
synagogues and in the corners of the streets, that they may be
seen of men. But thou, when thou prayest, enter into thy
closet, and when thou hast shut thy door, pray to thy Father
which is in secret *(Matthew 6:5, 6)*. In other words, retire to
the solitude of your humble home, look inward into the
deepest recesses of your heart, and take a careful and truthful
inventory of yourself in every department and detail. Ask
yourself earnestly whether you are trying to learn and obey
the law that governs your body. Ask yourself whether you are
living right, according to the mandates of the law; whether

you are bestowing upon your body that great degree of care and attention, which all men should give to the Temple of the Living God.

To look well to the care of the body is the first command of the Law-giver. To know how to care for the body is the first lesson of life. To neglect that duty is to commit the greatest crime against the Creator. The next care is to do naught that will injure the body of your neighbor.

Whether you have learned the first lesson of life and are putting in into practice, is quickly revealed by your state of health and the length of your years. For pain and misery, sickness and suffering, invalids and cripples, early decay and early death, are all the product of violated law. They are the direct result of sinning, as it were, against the Temple of the Living God. Christ made this clear in every case He healed. "Go and sin no more."

Divine Life is well pleased to remain active and long in the body of him who loves sufficiently strong its animating presence, to take the best care of the material form through which it flows and in which it abides on the visible plane. When the Christian religion has been revamped to a degree where it teaches this doctrine, instead of disregarding it as it now does, it will render humanity a real service.

Divine Life needs no savior. Save as long as you can by right living the Temple of Divine Life. You have nothing to do with Divine Life, for all that you are is the Divine Life flowing through your body.

The body is an instrument through which the individualized Spirit (Divine Life) contacts the earth plane. The Spirit is limited in its expression by the kind of a body in which it incarnates, and the condition of that body.

# Chapter No. 17
# What is the Soul?

After what has been said, it seems superfluous to refer especially to the so-called soul of man. Since Religionists have found much pleasure in preaching about the Human Soul, and of its eternal salvation or damnation hereafter, depending on the deportment of its possessor, it may be well to say something on the subject.

As to the "soul" Doctor Carver remarks:

"We are wont to speak of the Human Soul. *There is no such thing*. There is the Soul of the human being, but not the Human Soul.

"What do we mean by the Soul? We mean that the Soul is the indestructible part of a human being; that which we cannot conceive can die; that of which we cannot express death; that which, try as we may, we are entirely incapacitated to imagine can pass out of existence; the first cause of individual being, because it stands as the immediate cause of that which we know as separate existence; that which we conceive to be the core, the life, the intelligent force, causing all animation that we are capable of witnessing or realizing as taking place."

Soul, Spirit, Life, God, so far as we shall know, is interchangeable terms. They all mean the same thing. Yet few authors will agree to this. It is too simple and too easily understood. If such simplicity should go unchallenged and were believed in generally, religion, that baneful enslaver of man would lose its mystery and charm. For the veil of mysticism, in which religion is hidden, would be rent asunder; and then would disappear an institution that has caused millions to be murdered for God, and whose blood-curdling history runs back to the dawn of the race.

Let us review the matter more at length. It is written:

And the Lord God formed man of the dust of the ground and breathed into his nostrils the breath of life; and man became a living soul *(Genesis 2:7)*.

From certain kinds of material man constructs a locomotive engine. The engine sets on the track, a mass of inert steel. But it is so formed that it can move if conditions necessary for its movement are supplied. There might be an abundance of steam (life) all around the engine, but if none were in its boiler, it would have no effect on the engine. With the steam in the boiler, with the throttle open so that the steam may flow into the cylinders, the engine moves, and thus becomes, we might say, "a living soul."

The steam appears to bear the same relationship to the engine that the "breath of life" bears to man. It is the steam that makes the engine "a living soul;" it is the "breath of life" that makes man a "living soul." And that is all there is to it. We may call a man "a living soul" or a "living being," for the expression means no more.

The words which appear in *Genesis 2:7,* and are translated "living soul," are the identical words found in *Genesis 1:21*-24, but there translated "living creature." As to this change in the translation, W. E. Van Amburgh observes:

"If the Hebrew words are identically the same, we wonder why the translator of our King James Bible did not give the same rendering in the English! What authority had they to change it? We presume that they thought man should be called something different from other earthly beings.

"Mr. Isaac Leeser, a learned Jewish scholar, made a translation of the Old Testament front the original language to the English, which is very widely accepted by the English-speaking Jews. He renders the last clause of this verse: "And man became a living being." That is all there is in the statement (*The Way To Paradise*, page 63).

We wonder also why the translators of the Bible failed to give the same rendering in the English of the same words in the original language. And we feel that we have found the answer in Drummond's attempt to have a different "kind of life" build the various animal forms, then, as Solomon says, "a man hath no preeminence above a beast." And when Drummond's "soul" should arrive in "heaven," there would be found the "soul" of the mythical serpent of the Garden of Eden, and also "the released canine spirit" of the faithful dog, and so on. Again we read:

*"For what is a man profited, if he shall gain the whole world, and lose his soul?" (Matthew 16:26).*

According to Van Amburg, "the Greek word here rendered soul is 'psuche,' and is the only word in the New Testament translated soul. The same word is translated 'life' in the text: Arise, and take the young child and his mother, and go into the land of Israel: for they are dead which sought the young child's life (Greek, psuche)."

Here is more evidence of the willful turning, twisting, and warping of words, so as to give man a "soul." The attempt to build a "soul" for man, and prevent all other "living creatures" from having a "soul," has consumed as much time, labor, and thought, as the attempt to build on the teachings of Christ, the absurd doctrine of vicarious atonement, which we shall notice in a subsequent chapter. What reliance can be placed on teaching that deliberately deceives people in this manner?

Complexity and mystery generate the power that holds men in bondage. The failure of people to think, keeps them slaves to their leaders and rulers. For the thinker penetrates the veil of complexity and mystery, and comes to the center, where he finds simplicity and unity of cause.

The thinkers are the bearers of the Torch that drives before it the darkness of ignorance. When thinkers are allowed to work, tyrants tremble and nations fall. In all ages a few bold thinkers have infused hope and inspiration into a burdened and oppressed race. The little freedom which men now enjoy, has been bought and paid for in the blood of the thinker. It was the blood of the thinker that redeemed man from the horrible days of the Dark Ages; and it is the blood of Christ that redeemed a lost world from the curse of idolatry.

Of thinkers, Emerson remarks:

"Beware when the great God lets loose a thinker on this planet. Then all things are at risk. It is as when a conflagration has broken out in a great city, and no man knows what is safe, or where it will end. There is not a piece of science, but its flanks may be turned tomorrow; there is not any literary reputation, not the so-called eternal names of fame, that may not be reviled and condemned. The very hopes of man, the thoughts of his heart, the religion of nations, the manners and morals of mankind, are all at the mercy of a new generalization. Generalization is always a new influx of the divinity into the mind. Hence the thrill that attends it" (*Essays,* page 190).

Galileo and Copernicus were thinkers. They were cast into prison for daring to say that the world is round, when the priesthood was teaching that it was flat. Bruno was a thinker, and was burned because he found the common God of all Creation, and dared to give his "discovery" to a lost world. The priesthood claimed for them all knowledge regarding "God," and made the people believe that "God" had bestowed upon them the divine faculty of dominating nature in the curing of the sick, and in the saving of "souls." They could not save "souls," if there were none to save; and thus it was necessary for man, but not the other animals, to have a "soul."

Professor Doctor Hugo Magnus calls the wily priesthood the "servants of heaven." He observes:

"They made the people believe that all powers of the universe, the obvious ones as well as those mysteriously hidden in the depths of nature, were obedient to sacerdotal suggestions. The servants of heaven professed that they could regulate the eternal process of matter, with its becoming, being, and passing away, quite as irresistibly as their eye was able to survey the course of time in the past, present, and future.

"Equipped with these extensive powers, a priest necessarily appeared to the people not only as a physician, but also as a miraculous being crowned with the halo of the supernatural. And this was the role that he actually played in many ancient religions."

Bruno declared that God is in every blade of grass, in every grain of sand, and in every atom that floats in the sunshine. Such teaching could not be permitted, since it put the priesthood in an extremely embarrassing position. Furthermore, if believed by the people, it would strip and divest them of the power which held the people in bondage. And if such teaching were allowed, what would become of the doctrine of the "soul?" How could a "soul" that did not exist, be saved, or burned in eternal fire? — depending on the pleasure of the priesthood.

We lack space to go deeper into the matter of the willful turning, twisting, and warping of words and phrases in the Bible, in order to show how the Bible was compiled for the specific purpose of supporting certain phases of religious teaching. Sears, in his *History of the Bible,* 1844, pages *651, 665,* says:

"No less than 30,000 various readings of the Old and New Testaments have been discovered and putting alterations knowingly made, for the purpose of corrupting the text."

Reverend Professor Moses Stuart observes:

"In the Hebrew manuscripts that have been examined, some 80,000 various readings actually occur as to the Hebrew consonants. How many as to the vowel points and accents, no man knows" (*Critical History,* etc., page 192).

Doctor Alexander Winchell remarks:

"As to the standard Hebrew text, it is a fact of notoriety that the subdivisions into verses was not begun before the thirteenth century after Christ; that the Masoretic punctuation, including nearly all the vowels now employed in pronouncing the Hebrew, was not introduced till the period between the sixth and ninth century *after* Christ; that the separation of the text into words does not exist in the oldest manuscripts, and was effected not earlier than the tenth century after Christ; and that even the square-letter form of the radicals or consonants was not employed before the third century, after Christ" (*Pre-adamites,* page 9).

Clement Wood states:

"Sometime after the Babylonian captivity, then, certain priests made a final editing of the older narratives, reconciling them to some extent, and using only a fraction of the source of material. What was their dominant motive in this task? Why did they include some stories, and omit many more? What was the central idea controlling the whole work, which called for the inclusion of such diverse and apparently unrelated stories as the largely unexplained murder of Abel by Cain, the characteristics of Cain's descendants, the account of the city and tower of Babel, the destruction of the cities of Sodom and Gomorrah, the emphasis laid upon the oath of the Rechabites, and many others?

"Louis Wallis, in his *'Sociological Study of the Bible,'* has given the answer to these questions. He discovered that the Old Testament is an ethical collection, whose purpose was to pronounce moral judgments on past history, from a definite moral standpoint. Its purpose was not historical; the editors carelessly left in contradictions and discrepancies, and altered the records wherever this was necessary to fit their moralizing purpose.

"The collection was made to confirm the words of the great insurgent prophets, or preachers, who lived before the captivity and downfall of the nation. The editors made use of older Hebrew history and tradition just as far as this ancient material served their moralizing purpose, and no further. The controlling aim of the Old Testament is to advance the Yahweh religion as the worship of the One, righteous God, the God of a nomadic shepherd people, preached by their great preachers before the exile.

"The editors interspersed the ancient material with moral comments of their own, pointing out here and there their idea of the lessons of the selected past history that they included in the Old Testament" (*The Making Of The Old Testament,* page 9).

And this is a small part of the way in which was compiled the book, for a disputation of the contents of which thousands have been imprisoned, persecuted, murdered, burned, etc. Yea, men have suffered this for declaring that the Bible does not teach the doctrine of eternal torment.

Why should religious institutions tremble in the presence of truth? Why has religion never felt safe unless robed in a cloak of mystery? Why is it that things which can be understood, have never any place in religion? If a proposition appears reasonable and understandable, religion has always promptly rejected it, and persecuted those who advance it. Certainly the leaders of such a religion can be nothing more than dupes of their own belief; and the followers of it are the victims of ignorance, error, and confusion.

Truth is never confusing. It is error only that confuses us. Truth is always plain, simple, and understandable. Confusion arises not because truth is complex, but because of false belief. Belief in the result of teaching. The thing taught us may be right or wrong, but that has nothing to do with our belief.

The belief of humanity in general is the product of tradition, superstition, education, and environment. Truth has never been found in any of these sources, because truth makes men free, and the rulers have always seen well to it that humanity shall be kept in slavery.

It is the Soul (Divine Life) that builds the body, that animates the body, that thinks, sees, smells, feels, speaks, hears, tastes. It is the influx of Divine Life that makes man "a living soul (being)". His soul is his life, and his life is his God, as Christ clearly taught.

# Chapter No. 18
# The Mysterious Force

Nothing can rise higher than its source. Matter can never rise above the status of matter, regardless of how refined it may become. For "if the rivulet can flow but one inch higher than the sufficiency of its cause, there is no reason why it should not climb the mountain-top, and 'increase by force of its own intensity,' as the medical doctor says of disease" (Walter).

If man is entirely the product of matter, it must follow that he is limited in his capacity by that which has produced him. If man is the product of matter only, he can rise no higher than the limits of matter. Therefore, if the force that animates the form of man, is the result of a chemical formula, then it must follow that this force, in every particular and in every detail, is limited always and forever by that which has produced it.

But every day of our life, even as a toddling child, we raise superior to matter — superior to any chemical formula or any chemical reaction. We perform conduct that matter cannot perform. We think thoughts that matter cannot think — thoughts that cannot originate in matter. We receive knowledge which does not abide in matter, and which matter can neither receive nor impart. And we rise to the conception of the highest pinnacle, and conceive of the Creator and Ruler of the Universe. Were we the product of matter only, these marvelous functions we could never exercise?

We have observed that in the Universe there is a mysterious something, which we cannot define, which appears to be inexplicable, but without which we could not move, nor speak, no see, nor smell, nor feel, nor hear; without which, to us, there would be no light, no sound, no heat, no cold, nor, indeed, terrestrial life, and our bodies would be as dead as the dust of Judas. What this mysterious something is, no man knows; but that it is, no man can dispute. It is not demonstrable to the senses, and it is with great difficulty that so-called science can be persuaded that it exists at all.

By the use of material language, we cannot express the spiritual. By thinking material thoughts, we cannot conceive of the spiritual. That is why we cannot define Divine Life; that is why we cannot conceive of Divine Life. In our material way we think of it and call it God, Deity, Soul, Spirit, First Cause, and so on. These terms mean nothing. They define nothing, nor describe anything that we can understand. But regardless of what we think of it, or of the name by which we call it, there is a mysterious, elusive something, which is the equal and sufficient cause of all that occurs, from the building of a gnat to the construction of a prophet, from the creation of a grain of sand to the creation of worlds.

Divine Life is the mysterious force that animates man. All that he is, results from Divine Life flowing through his body. Divine Life is the force that produces man and all the functions of his body, from smelling to seeing, from feeling to minding. It produces the brain to think with, and produces thoughts in the brain. It generates in the brain that wonderful faculty called the mind, so that man may be impressed with the same attributes possessed by the Maker.

How this can be, you say. Since the Maker is infinite, the attributes of the Maker must be infinite. That is correct. But since all that man appears to express, is merely the expression of Divine Life through his body, it follows that the attributes which he appears to have, are really the attributes of the Maker. So the attributes of the Maker, while infinite, are finite so far as man is concerned, for the reason that the human mind is limited by the capacity of the material brain; and the Infinite Attributes of the Maker, which man appears to express, are necessarily limited by his limited capacity to receive them, and not by the capacity of the Maker to impart them. And in proportion as a man grows in truth, and casts off the false, degrading, material education which restricts and limits his capacity of receptivity, in the same degree does he increase his receptive powers; and when in this respect he rises above material limitations, he becomes an immaculate Christ that declares to a lost world:

Whosoever eateth my flesh and drinketh my blood, hath (now) eternal life; and I (truth) will raise him up at the last day (the day that the material and the spiritual man part) *(John 6:54)*.

That is what we call Inspiration. When a man is *free* from the creeds and chains of a dogmatic religion, when he is not bound by the dogma of material education, when he can gaze into the blade of grass and the grain of sand and *see* Divine Life, into his heart flows a flood of light that clears his understanding of the fog and haze in which is lost the lord of the visible realm.

How ridiculous to hear of tales in which is expressed the belief in a "visitation" from a personal God. In the Maison de Detention at Bern; Doctor Francis Joseph Gall saw a religious fanatic, who believed that Christ, surrounded by a brilliant light, as though a million of suns had combined their splendors, had appeared to him to reveal the true religion. Our literature is filled with stories of similar kind. Nor do we seem able to rise above this deluding condition. Reverend Doctor John Roach Stratton says that his son received "a visitation from God." The account is related in the press of June 25, 1927, as follows:

"At an all-night prayer meeting in Calvary Baptist church, Stratton said that his son, Warren, 19 years old, whom he ordained as a Baptist minister last year, lay prone on the floor at the end of a prayer, uttered unintelligible words and sang so beautifully that his parents believed, Stratton said, that he had a 'visitation from God.'"

According to such views, to prove "a visitation from God," all one need do is to "lay prone on the floor and utter unintelligible words." Things that can be understood never emanate from "God," nor from a religion that worships "God." It is the unintelligible mutterings of idiocy and insanity that indicate the receipt of message from "God."

From the stinking fumes of decaying matter comes life, and from the mutterings of insanity come the messages of life (God). Even the light of an immaculate Christ is too dim to dispel the darkness of a world lost in the depths of such blasting ignorance.

# Chapter No. 19
# What is Intuition?

Why does man believe in the existence of a Supreme Being? No race has been found that did not entertain this belief. On what is it based? Since the belief is universal, it must come from a universal source, through a universal channel, be received by a universal faculty, and be interpreted in a universal manner. What is the secret of this great university? There can be but one answer — Intuition.

The Inspired Men of history were men who developed, consciously or unconsciously, the faculty of intuition. Aside from their conception arising from observation, comparison, reflection, and memory, they had that instinctive intuitive impulse which led them to look into the "kingdom of God within," and there they found that God (Divine Life) is truly in every blade of grass and every grain of sand. They discovered this truth because they rose above the narrow limit of material being, and thus increased the capacity of their receptivity of knowledge flowing into them from the Infinite Source.

This is the mysterious channel through which comes the mysterious and inexplicable information that man was not brought into the world to grow old and die, as do the beasts of the field. Man now thinks in his heart that he should so die; but the still, small voice of Intuition keeps whispering that it is not true. He listens and he faintly believes for a time, but he soon forgets. There comes another who listens and believes more firmly, and who investigates that belief. His findings he publishes to a lost world. He is burned; and ages afterwards his findings become the foundation of a new civilization.

If man were required to prove that he is brought into the world to grow old and die, as do the beasts, how would he do it? He could not prove it by experience, for has not all experience shown the contrary?

If it were necessary to prove the existence of a Supreme Being, how would we proceed to do it? If we should attempt to prove any of the great truths of the Universe, how would we proceed to do it? It could be done only by and through that unexplainable faith or feeling which transcends human conception — through Intuition.

Doctor W. F. Warren remarks:

"All religions, if traced back, will be found rooted in a single fact: the soul's instinctive, fundamental, ineradicable feeling or conviction, that it stands in a real relation to piety and that this relation is capable of conscious and continuous realization by action, the adoration of an idol, the burning of a beast, the offering of a prayer."

It is the same "instinctive, fundamental, ineradicable feeling or conviction" of the "soul" that makes man feel that he was not brought into the world to grow old and die as do the beasts. From whence does the "soul" derive or receive this "instinctive, fundamental, ineradicable feeling or conviction?" We shall see.

The great Truths of the Universe cannot be proved by experience and demonstration. The truths proclaimed by the "inspired men" of the past, were not based on experience and demonstration. Indeed, all experience and demonstrable evidence proved just the contrary to what they taught. The sun did revolve around the earth, for could not people see it with their own eyes? The great Truths of the Universe are received into the mind of man from the Infinite Source, through the mysterious, universal channel of Intuition; and the men who have listened to them, and believed in them, and died for them, we say of these immortal lights that they were INSPIRED.

What is Intuition? It is the involuntary promptings, received into the conscience without apparent effort, which inspire men and spur them onward, without apparent thought or reason, contrary to all information and evidence furnished by experience and demonstration, and in the face of certain ridicule, persecution, and death. It is Divine Intelligence flowing from Divine Life into the mind; and when received by the mind, and recognized by man, then it is that such men become Inspired, and are able to look into infinite space and infinite time, and perceive the truth as it is, and not as a wicked world would have it.

Doctor Warren says that it is the soul's instinctive, fundamental, ineradicable feeling or conviction that it stands in a real relation to Diety. But we say that it is the Divine Inspiration that arises from the "kingdom of God within," and comes to man when he casts off the material limitations of a lost world, which binds him in slavery to material thoughts. It is the truth that makes men free from the restricting and blighting influences of their limiting beliefs.

Intuition is the window of the Soul, through which the Spiritual part of man gazes far out beyond the horizon of human discord and error, and perceives in the vast distance, and implants in the consciousness of the few thinking individuals who appear in each generation, the brilliant light of Truth. These persons are able to visualize, in all its dazzling glory, a wondrous image of the continuous and harmonious state of Perpetual Youth, which was originally man's, on condition that he obey the law, and which he forfeited by deliberate disregard of the law.

Of Intuition, Professor O. S. Fowler remarks:

"Discerning universal truth is another of its (Intuition's) functions and that still more important. Since it reads men, why not also other truths equally. Intuitive perception of universal truth from little data is its specialty; Men certainly do possess this gift; and some to a much greater extent than others. In some the merest inkling suffices to put them upon the track; when they jump instantly and correctly to results. It scents truth as the hound scents the fox, and approaches it, not by labored ratiocination, nor induction, nor deduction, but by intellectual inspiration and intuitive discernment.

"We have seen man's need and possession of spiritual intuition; he equally needs intellectual inspiration — some window to his mind opening out above towards all truth, through which it may enter his understanding to expand and feed his soul." (*Human Science,* page 1134).

Doctor Carver says some interesting things about Intuition. We shall quote him:

"We are limited in our acquisition of knowledge to intuition — deduction. There is no other, there has never been another, there will never be another channel through which we may receive universal intelligence. We must get universal truth, if at all, through intuition.

"And the statement last made does not negative any form of religion that exists in the world today. For if any Bible is truth, the substance of that truth was transmitted through the process of intuition.

"Intuition — deduction, is the only way that universal intelligence may be transmitted to us. It is the only way that it has ever been transmitted; the only way it can ever be transmitted. These statements become perfectly clear, when we look the situation squarely in the face; for you will understand that all the religions of the world hold that they obtained their basic principles from the God of the Universe, called by whatever name, which is, after all, nothing but the transmission from the Great Soul, of the universal truth through the process of intuition to human beings.

"How does universal truth come to us? It comes through all of the multifold avenues of our being that have been described in this course of lectures; that is to say, through tissue sense, common sensation, and special sensation. It also comes through our four other senses, and this is but the equivalent of saying, that is comes through all media of suggestion."

Doctor Carver may not have fully realized it at the time, but he shows by his observations that he was, perhaps unconsciously, feeling for the same "fountain of youth" when he was inspired to make his remarks regarding the peculiar influence of the power of Premonition. We use the word "inspired" advisedly, for no man could find it in his power to say what Doctor Carver is about to say, were he not influenced by an inspiration that comes only from Universal Truth. He says:

"There is a way by which knowledge of events that have not yet taken place, it is said, may be known, through what is called premonition. As to this phenomenon, I desire to say, by way of explanation, that the transmission of intelligence of this character by premonition, is the most difficult for us to understand of any that has been referred to, or discussed. And this is true because we have been so definitely and carefully schooled to our material limitations. The impossibility of acquiring knowledge of events before they occur, through a means common to all, has always been carefully and most impressively taught to us.

"However, if you believe that God is possessed of omniscience, omnipotence, and omnipresence, and that your Soul possesses those powers potentially, you must also believe that God's knowledge is from the beginning; is comprehensive of everything, and that your Soul, having these powers in potentiality, is possessed of the means of receiving all knowledge. Believing in the named God attributes, you must also believe that an event which has not yet taken place is as much a part of universal truth as though it had occurred. And, therefore, under the very most favorable circumstances, you must admit that your Soul may receive from the Great Soul a fragment of such truth, comprising some event that has not yet been enacted, and evolve it into your consciousness.

"You would not expect such an immaculate event to occur in every life, or to occur with any degree of frequency, but you would expect that, under the exactly proper circumstances, such transmission would take place" (*Psycho-Bio-Physiology*, page 118).

The knowledge of the Great Soul is also the knowledge of the Soul of man, and vice versa. If we believe the knowledge of the Great Soul is from the beginning, we must believe that the Soul of man has the potential capacity to receive knowledge from the beginning. If we believe this, then we "must also believe that an event which has not yet taken place is as much a part of universal truth as though it had occurred."

# Chapter No. 20
# The Voice of the Soul

If there be no soul, how can it have a voice? But what name shall we give to that peculiar force, feeling, impulse, within each individual, urging him to do right? In man it is said to be the Conscience. In animals we call it instinct. Every living creature, regardless of how low in the scale of life, is able to recognize, anticipate, and supply its needs. The tiny insects, the worms, the fowls, the beasts, yea, even the vegetable kingdom — all these are able to recognize, anticipate, and supply their needs. All these seem to know how to control their conduct and direct their efforts that their well-being may be promoted, and their existence preserved and perpetuated. Shall we say that these forms, down to the lowest we can think of, possess in and of themselves the uncanny intelligence they appear to exhibit?

Let us observe this from another angle. In the autumn the migratory birds in the northland, gather in great flocks at various points, and chirp and chatter as though in important conference. Within a few days the feathered flocks wing their way toward the warm skies of the sunny south, and spend the dreary months of winter in the balmy temperature of the tropics and semi-tropics.

Perchance, half of the birds had never been there before. They were hatched out during the early summer in various sections of the northern forests. They know nothing of winter; they know nothing of the southland. How can they foretell that frost and snow and ice are coming, and that they must travel in a certain direction, to escape being starved and frozen to death? What do the birds know about the points of the compass? How do they know which way to go in order to avoid cold winter's icy blast?

But, you say, the younger birds are directed and led by the older ones, who have been through the experience before, and thus know what *is* coming and what course to take to evade it. This does not solve the problem, for the result would be the same if all the older birds were killed off, and none left but those hatched out during the summer in the northern woods. Going farther, we find the same uncanny intelligence directing and guiding the entire animal world. The ant and the bee labor during the summer to lay up provisions to carry them thru the winter. The new-born pig at once seeks its mother's breast for nourishment; and for the same purpose the new-born calf seeks the udder of the cow. The apparently insensate acorn falls to the ground, and when proper conditions are supplied, it sends forth a sprout which bifurcates, one fork shooting up into the air, and the other going down into the soil.

What influence directs all this conduct? Shall we, with the Evolutionist, call it the blind, unreasoning force of Nature? Or shall we, with the Religionist, call it the divine guidance of a personal God of wrath, anger, repentance, love, and so on? Joseph Mc Cabe says respecting this:

"It is sometimes said, especially by Sir Oliver Lodge, that the argument can be entirely changed, and restored to its full strength, by admitting that natural causes produced everything, but that God guided these natural agencies. You might, for instance, trace in science the whole series of movements, from the primitive nebula onward, which eventually produced the bee, with all its wonderful 'instincts.' But, Sir Oliver, you would not see the guidance of these natural agencies by a supernatural power.

"Yes, quite naturally. What Sir Oliver forgets is that he has to prove that there was such guidance. He can do this only by proving that such guidance was necessary: that the natural agencies of evolution would not have produced the bee, as we know it, unless they were guided. I have repeatedly challenged him to prove this, and he has never done it. It cannot be done.

"Moreover, this idea of 'guidance' of the forces of nature, which is very popular with some, raises a score of difficulties the moment you examine it closely. How would you guide a billiard ball, without pushing it? Can a mind communicate its designs to matter, and could matter carry out such designs if they were communicated? Do the atoms in the rose know that they are working out a design? In what earthly sense can anyone conceive these atoms to be guided" (*Futility Of Belief In God,* page 29).

If McCabe knew what Christ meant when he said, It is the spirit that quickeneth the flesh profiteth nothing — he would have nothing to say about "the natural agencies of evolution producing the bee." These so-called agencies have produced nothing. All that is, so far as we know, is the product of Divine Life, operating on and through matter. "The natural agencies" themselves are the product of Divine Life, and would disappear into invisible gas in the twinkling of an eye, were the sustaining influence of Divine Life withdrawn from them for an instant.

If he had understood the words of "Spirit and of Life," Mc-Cube would have said nothing about "mind communicating its designs to matter." He would have known that matter is dead; that matter never lives; that matter does nothing of itself, nor by virtue of its own power; for matter has no power, it has nothing, and under certain conditions it is decomposed and dissipated into the invisible realms, beyond the reach of human vision.

The "instinct" that guides the bee is not instinct at all. It is a certain intelligence that the bee appears to possess, yet does not possess. It is this intelligence that guides the bird; and never yet has this intelligence betrayed a living creature that has trusted it. For instance, the condition that the birds hope to find in the south, is there. But how do the birds know that? Has the "natural agencies of evolution" that produced them, impressed this intelligence on their material bodies, or communicate this intelligence to their material brains?

"How would you guide a billiard ball, without pushing it?" We suspect that the "natural agencies of evolution" guide the birds by pushing them. The "natural agencies of evolution" know just when the birds should go south, and guide the birds south at the proper time by "pushing" their bodies in that direction. How strange those brilliant men will spend their lives groping in such darkness, and become so engrossed in their labor as to be unable to see the absurdity of their belief.

The uncanny intelligence that guides birds and bees in their journey through life, is "the voice of the soul." The mysterious impulse that tells man right from wrong, and urges him to do right is "the voice of the soul."

Birds, bees, and all creatures below man, have not the ability to cast off and disregard the divine influence — "the voice of the soul." So lacking the ability to violate the law of their being, they live in harmony with their environment and enjoy the blessings intended should be theirs. They are not mocked in their efforts. And men marvel at the "instinct" displayed by animals, and are so dull as to ascribe it to the "natural agencies of evolution." Such dense ignorance; when will they see the light?

The same intelligence that so unerringly guides the animal world flows also into the mind of man. And man, with his vastly superior abilities and capacities, could use that intelligence to raise himself far above the birds and bees, if he would. He could use his greater endowments to learn the mysteries of the Law of Life, and use to great advantage the knowledge thus gained. But the law that he should know so well, is an utter stranger to him; and when mention is made of such a law, he lifts his eyebrows in amazement.

So he blunders on in his blind course, lost in a sea of ignorance, groping in darkness, wandering in the wilderness, struggling against an environment which should be in harmony with him, but which is hostile instead because his own perverse conduct has made it so.

His many miseries arising from his violation of the law of which he knows nothing, he lays to demons, devils, and germs. And the great intellect that he was given to learn and know the law, he uses in his efforts to try to escape the penalty of his transgressions of the law.

# Chapter No. 21
# The Divine Life

Since there is no life but Divine Life; likewise, there is no intelligence but Divine Intelligence. And since Divine Intelligence is infinite and omniscient, therefore Divine Intelligence knows precisely the climatic conditions of Florida as well as of North Dakota, of Mexico as well as of Canada, of South America as well as of North America, of the Eastern Hemisphere as well as of the Western Hemisphere.

As the living existence of all forms, whether vegetal or animal, birds or bees, monkeys or men, is but an expression of Divine Life through such forms, it follows that the intelligence, apparently possessed by such forms, is in reality an expression of Divine Intelligence through the form. In other words, all intelligence is Divine Intelligence, for apart from Divine Intelligence there is no intelligence, just as apart from Divine Life there is no life. But, you say, if the intelligence expressed by a living form is Divine Intelligence, and as Divine Intelligence is Infinite Intelligence, why the intelligence is expressed by a particular form not Infinite Intelligence. That is a good point, and we shall give it special notice.

We have said that Divine Life rigidly observes the Law of Economy. No animal is endowed beyond its needs, and none are given less than its needs require. Every living creature is endowed with capacity to receive from the Unlimited Source, sufficient intelligence to enable it to live in the environment in which it is placed, but no more and no less. Less would be insufficient, and would soon lead to the extinction of the animal; and more would be superfluous, since the animal would have no need for it, could not use it, and that would mean waste. This never occurs in anything nor anywhere throughout the entire Universe, since Economy is a law that rules the conduct of Divine Life.

Divine Intelligence, although infinite, is finite so far as all living things are concerned. It is finite because they are finite. It is limited to them because their capacity to receive and use it is limited. It is the capacity of the animal to receive intelligence, and not the capacity of the Creator to bestow it, that determines the amount of intelligence which shall be expressed by and through each particular form, whether it be men, beasts, birds, bees, and so on.

Birds possess no individual intelligence. That is to say, of themselves birds have no intelligence, no more than have bees and beasts and men. They know not north from south, nor east from west. But they are directed in their course by Divine Life through the influence of what is called animal instinct. There is no such thing as "animal instinct." For so-called animal instinct is nothing more nor less than the expression of Divine Intelligence through animal forms, just as what we call living is nothing more nor less than the expression of Divine Life through animal forms.

The conditions that the birds hope to find in the south are there, and the birds know it — not because the "natural agencies of evolution" have impressed any "instinct" upon their material frame; they know it because their intelligence is that part of Divine Intelligence which they have capacity to express, just as their life is that part of Divine Life which their particular form has capacity to express.

# Chapter No. 22
# Why Men Are Mocked

Are men less endowed than other creatures? If the favorable conditions those birds hope to find in the south are there, and the birds know it, and go and find it, shall we say that the conditions of perpetual youth, which man is incessantly seeking and someday hopes to find, do not exist; that it is a myth, the dream of a diseased mind, the reaction of humanity to a natural impulse, which is the dread of the infirmities of age and the horror of death? Shall birds follow the promptings of "animal instinct," or Intuition, and find that for which they search, while men are mocked in their efforts?

We cannot believe this. We cannot believe that we are less endowed than other animals. On the other hand, our endowment is far greater. It is, in fact, so great that it has made blind fools of men. It has made them think that they are Life, and they will not see that they are not Life.

The intelligence possessed by birds, is only that part of Divine Intelligence which their very limited capacity is constructed to receive. But it is sufficient to enable them to live in the environment in which they are placed by the influence of the Divine Will. Since birds have no will power but that of Divine Life, in their conduct we behold the marvelous operation of Divine Will Power, exercised without restriction by material limitations.

Man, being endowed with powers not bestowed upon other animals, is able to disregard the influence of the Divine Will. He has a will of his own, and has used it exclusively to his detriment. Instead of using his will in conjunction and co-operation with the Divine Will, and thus improve his condition, he has used it to subvert and obstruct his course, and is so blind as to believe that this is "progress."

Man reaps what he sows, and Solomon must have beheld this reaping and sowing when he said:

*For in much wisdom is much grief; and he that increased knowledge increased sorrow. Lo, this only have I found, that God, hath made man upright; but they have sought out many inventions (Ecclesiastes 1:18 and 7:29).*

Something is sadly wrong when much wisdom means much grief, and the increase of knowledge is the increase of sorrow. It means wisdom and knowledge of the wrong kind; it means wisdom and knowledge that lead in the wrong direction; it means wisdom and knowledge that subvert and obstruct the true course of things and produce the innumerable "inventions" that men have made in their silly efforts to improve on Nature. When the weight of their "inventions" begins to crush them, they call for help and cry out, O Father, save me! And they clutch at the doctrine of a false religion which holds, that man is redeemed through the blood of a rejected and murdered Christ.

"Science is remaking our lives," pipes a lost and silly world. Yes, indeed, Science is the serpent in the Garden of Eden, and some day this fact man will discover. When he does, and casts science into the pit of eternal darkness, then he will also discover his relationship to his Maker, and recover many of the blessings which he once enjoyed, but lost when by his inventions he set out to improve on Nature.

To improve on Nature means to violate the law. For to improve on Nature means to subvert, obstruct, and change the true course of things. In thousands of ways man violates the law, and calls this "improving on Nature." For his pains he has much grief and sorrow. He has increased sickness and suffering, and from a life-span of a thousand years, he has reduced his days to less than half a century on the average. And he still continues his search for the "fountain of youth," by means of which he hopes to recover that which through his wickedness he has lost.

The "fountain of youth" is not a myth. It is a reality. In every age, men have searched for it, and poets have sung of it. And Doctor Carver may deny it, but he was thinking of it when he made his marvelous statements. Perpetual youth is "an event which has not yet taken place;" therefore, no man could think of such an occurrence; for man cannot call before his mind the image of that which has no existence, never had existed, and could never have existed. Hence, the thought of perpetual youth could not have occurred to man, were it not for the fact that —

"Your Soul may receive from the Great Soul a fragment of such truth, comprising some event that has not yet been enacted, and evolve it into your consciousness."

Ralph Waldo Emerson was another profound thinker, who often freed his mind of the limitations of material bondage, and gazed beyond the apparent rim of sky and sea, penetrating the unknown kingdom that cannot be reached by the human eye or ear. On one occasion while influenced by the inspiration that comes only from within, he wrote:

"My hope for the human race is bright as the morning star; for a glory is coming to man such as the most inspired tongues of prophets and poets, have never been able to describe."

Again he says:

"If you gather apples in the sunshine, or make hay, or hoc corn, and then retire within doors, and shut your eyes, and press them with your hand, you shall still see apples hanging in the bright light, with boughs and leaves thereto, or the tasseled grass, or the corn flags, and this for five or six hours afterwards.

"There lie the impressions on the retentive organs, though you knew it not. So lies the whole series of natural images with which your life has made you acquainted, in your memory, though you know it not, and a thrill of passion flashes light on their dark chamber, and the active power seizes instantly the fit image, as the word of its momentary thought."

To find truth, we must search within, and not without. We must close our eyes, drive all material limitations from our mind, and place ourselves in perfect rapport with the Divine Life. It is then only that a thrill of passion flashes into the deepest recesses of our being, and inspires us with a feeling that no language can paint and no pen portray.

When we assume this attitude, then our Soul, which is the Divine Life, receives from the Great Soul, the Source of Divine Life, the impression of eternal youth; and by the power of intuition, this impression is communicated to the mind, and the mind translates the impression into thoughts. Otherwise such thoughts could never come into the mind.

The reason why so few men will trust themselves to believe in these thoughts is because all past experience appears to refute the fact of eternal youth. But such testimony is unreliable and faulty, because man's conduct has always been faulty, and because his education has always been wrong.

All men, through the Soul, have access to primary truth; and all men have some capacity to receive it. But only in the open mind, free from the limitations fixed by school education and materialistic belief, does primary truth find lodgment; and in such minds, which are few indeed, it produces inspirations that make men seers and prophets.

# Chapter No. 23
# Death the Penalty of Disobedience

There are many who think that man should not die and leave this world as he does. Sonic hold that man, for reasons which we propose to relate somewhat in detail in another place, should not see death, nor be ill, nor feel physical pain — that he should not experience the sorrow and suffering with which his home has been filled from the earliest recorded times. And we are told that a day will come when these distressing conditions shall pass away *(Revelation 21:4)*.

In discussing the question, let us revert to the Bible. This great library of books contains a record of what purports to be the creation of all things of which we have any knowledge. However, we do not desire to be understood as believing that creation occurred as stated in the Bible.

From the evidence obtainable, it appears that the Bible account of creation was "written by Moses, during the forty-year wanderings of the Children of Israel in the wilderness, between the years 1615 and 1575 before Christ" *(Van Am burgh)*. No man will ever know how creation occurred, and certainly Moses did not know.

The story related in the Bible asserts that by one-man sin entered into the world, and death by sin; and that the wages of sin is death *(Romans 5:12)*. In other words, if sin were removed from man, death would disappear, since death depends on sin, and if the cause be removed the effect could not exist. Before taking up the question of sin, in order to ascertain just how it is or can be responsible for death, let us see whether eternal life in the flesh is possible. Can Life decay and die? No. Life itself contains within itself no principle of either decay or death. There is no reason that can be explained from a biological or anatomical standpoint, why the human body should not continue on and on forever.

"There is no physiological reason at the present day why man should die," says Doctor William A. Hammond, late Surgeon General of the U. S. Army. Death is not a primitive attribute of animated matter *(Weismann)*. The human frame is apparently intended to go on forever *(Munroe)*. There is no physiological nor biological reason for death *(Claunch)*.

Since the findings of biologists, physiologists, and anatomists are agreed without exception, that no reason exists why the body should not continue on and on, then the cause of the body's dissolution must be located in some other direction, since that cause does not seem to be in the body itself.

"The wages of sin is death," declared Paul. What did he mean? Did he himself know exactly of the profound principle that lay back of that assertion? If the wages of sin is death, and if death means the dissolution of the body, there must be back of this proposition far more than appears on its face. In order for sin to destroy the body, sin must affect the body in some specific manner. It must generate a destructive process within the body. For if I curse my neighbor, fail to pay my debts, or even blaspheme against the so-called Holy Ghost, that of itself should have no degenerative influence on my physical frame, since its well-being and continuation depend upon more-weighty and more material things than curses, payments of debts, and blasphemy.

It is true, however, that the body may be destroyed by adverse mental conditions, resulting from fear, fright, worry, jealousy, anger, etc., which so influence the body's function as to cause it to become abnormal, thus resulting in decay of the body. And the mental state may become so acute adversely, as to result in sudden death — as in the case of Richard Barrett, 60 years old, of Aberdeen, Washington, who on May 21, 1927, dropped dead on the street from intense excitement; it is said, at the news of Captain Charles Lindbergh's safe arrival in Paris in his flight from New York. The press of June 18, 1927, states that Robert Moser, 18 years old, ill with appendicitis, died on the operating table from "sudden dilation of the heart, caused by extreme mental suffering and the fear that he would die," according to the statement of his physicians.

But the Great Sin that is described in the third chapter of Genesis, to which consistent reference is subsequently directed by the men of the Bible, and to which Paul referred, but the nature of which he did not appear to understand, is not that which primarily affects the mind. The sin that entered into the world by one man, and death by sin, is not that sin which ministers of the gospel find pleasure in expounding to a credulous people, kept in the dark by miss-education.

The sin here involved, and the sin that we shall notice in the next chapter, is a sin that primarily affects the integrity of the body, and subsequently affects the mind by deteriorating the organ that produces the mind. An abnormal brain must produce an abnormal mind, and a normal brain the Divine Life cannot construct from defective building material.

The Great Sin, the sin committed against the Temple of the Living God, is a sin that is committed daily, and many times each day, not only by doctors of divinity, and doctors of drugs, and doctors of all kinds and descriptions, but by every man that ever lived, from the first to the present day.

The sin that Adam committed is daily committed by the most devout so-called Christians; and yet it is never noticed nor thought of by the most zealous evangelist. It is here that all religions fail, including the Christian. A religion that does not teach the Law of Life, that does not teach men how to live for health and strength, that does not direct men how to preserve and protect the Temple of the Living God, is a religion that does not meet the most elementary requirements of humanity.

When theologists cease splitting hairs, when they discard their wild fancies in their search of God, and in their efforts to "save the soul," and begin to search for fundamental facts, they will discover what sin is. Then, if they are influenced by love for humanity, instead of the greed for gold, they will begin to render the suffering world a beneficial service — the only purpose of religion and the only one that it has failed to perform.

# Chapter No. 24
# The Great Commandment

Then one of the scribes (a lawyer) came, and having heard them reasoning together, and perceiving that he (Christ) had answered them well, asked Him, saying, Master, which is the great commandment in the Law? *(Mark 12:28)*.

The Master, unquestionably being much surprised at the display of such inexcusable ignorance, promptly replied by quoting a statement that had been made fifteen centuries before. And Jesus answered him:

Hear, O Israel: The Lord our God is one Lord; and thou shalt love the Lord thy God with all thine heart, and with all thy soul, and with all thy might *(Deuteronomy 6:4-5; 10:12)*. This is the first and great commandment *(Matthew 22:37, 38; Mark 12:29, 30)*.

God is Divine Life. He alone hath Life in Himself; for all live unto Him *(John 4:24; Luke 20:38)*. And in Him we live, and move, and have our being *(Acts 17:28)*.

The home of Divine Life, so far as man is concerned, is the Temple of the Living God, the Kingdom of God within you *(Luke 17:21)*. When we feel the heartbeat, when we hear soft strains of sweet music, smell the perfume-ladened air, when we see the glories of the Universe, remember that man is not Life *(John 6:63)*, that man can do nothing of himself *(John 15:5);* that man's existence is not separate from the existence of the Creator. Embrace the whole truth by acknowledging that in Him, the Divine Life, we live, and move, and have our being.

Our material body is the visible home of the most majestic power, the most mysterious force, known. In this home that force, the Divine Life, the Great Spirit, will tarry with joy and pleasure, just as long as the home, by its deportment, is and remains a suitable and worthy abode for the King of kings and the Lord of lords.

Since man is the highest form which the Divine Life has constructed from the material world, and since it is only fitting that the Creator should bestow upon His masterpiece the blessedness and happiness of a perfect existence, He gave to man a power which He withheld from all other creatures. That power is the Intellect, about which more shall be said in the proper place.

By the use of his intellect, man alone was given the capacity to understand his relation to his Creator, and to comprehend the law, which is written in the inward parts of his physical frame *(Jerimiah 31:33)*. What a wonderful world this would be to live in, if man used his intellect as he should.

To impress more vividly upon the mind of man, that his first and greatest care is that of protecting and preserving his body, which is constantly wasting and wearing away, and as constantly being repaired and rebuilt, his attention was specifically drawn to the fact, that the only way he could destroy his body was to neglect and abuse it. By the use of defective building material, the body would be improperly nourished, and it would decay and disintegrate. So man was solemnly admonished, commanded, that in the day that he failed to furnish his body with proper building material, his physical frame would begin to degenerate, and "dying thou shalt die."

Let us consider this phase of the subject somewhat briefly with Pastor Russell. In defining the words "immortal" and "mortal," he observes:

"Adam was created mortal — in a condition in which death was a possibility or everlasting life a possibility;

according as he pleased or displeased his wise, just, and loving Creator. Had he remained obedient, he would have continued living until now — and forever — and yet all the while he would have been moral, liable to death if disobedient.

"Nor would such a condition be one of uncertainty; for God with whom he had to do is unchangeable; hence, Adam would have had full assurance of everlasting life so long as he continued loyal and obedient to his Creator. And more than this could not reasonably be asked.

"Adam's life condition previous to his disobedience was similar to that now enjoyed by the holy angels: he had life in full measure — lasting life — which he might have retained forever by remaining obedient to God. But because he was not death-proof, because he did not have 'life in himself,' but was dependent for continuance upon conditions subject to his Creator's pleasure, therefore God's threat that if he disobeyed he should die, meant something. It meant the loss of the spark of life, 'the breath of life,' without which the body would molder into dust, and the living soul or sentiment being would cease" (*The Atonement etc.*, page 391).

In what did Adam fail to remain obedient to God? In that he failed to supply his body with the building material the Father had provided for him. Of this Pastor Russell says:

"The conditions of life are explained to us as having been a special grove of life-giving trees, by the eating of which man's life would have continued, making good daily its wastes, and suffering no decay. As soon as man became a transgressor, he was restrained from access to these trees of life, or orchard of life, and thus, like the lower animals of his dominion, became subject to death. In man's case, however, death is said to be a 'curse'" (The *Atonement, etc.*, page 400).

Let us pause here and correct a couple of errors we have quoted: (1) The "living soul" never "ceases" to be. The reader knows this, if he has followed us closely. The "living soul" is the "living life," which had no beginning and has no end. (2) There are no "life-giving trees," and there were never any such trees. All things that liveth are animated by Divine Life. There is no other life. Nothing can give life. God does not give life. He alone is life, Divine Life, and Divine Life, which is given to nothing, expresses itself through innumerable varieties of forms, and departs when the forms are no longer a suitable place for the indwelling of Divine Life.

The fruit of the tree is the perfect building material for the human frame. If the human frame be furnished with perfect building material, in the right quantity, and the owner of the frame obey all the other laws of life, there would be no end of his existence in the flesh, for Divine Life never departs from the body until the body becomes an unsuitable place for its habitation.

The "tree of life" mentioned in *Genesis 3:22, 24,* could be no other kind of a tree, than that which would supply perfect building material to repair man's constantly wasting frame. We might indeed call it the "tree of life," if a man ate thereof and never died. He would think it a "tree of life." To all appearances it would then be a "tree of life." But in fact it would be a tree that furnished the body with perfect building material, and not with "life."

Getting back. How does the "curse" operate in order to produce death? The stability and integrity of the body are destroyed for the want of proper building material — the very thing we have been discussing. Again Pastor Russell says:

"Viewing man as a whole (mentally, morally, and physically one) as the Scriptures do, we can see that the curse, the sentence of death, is in operation against every part and element of his being; and looking about us throughout the world, we find corroboration of this on every hand. As, in the decay of physical powers, the weakest point with some is the stomach, with others the muscles, with others the bones, so in viewing man as a whole, we find that in some the greatest loss, decay, depravity, has been mental, with others moral, with others, physical, yet all are blemished in all respects; all were hopelessly 'lost' under this curse" (*The Atonement, etc.,* page 408).

In spite of the deteriorating effect of wrong building material, the first men were so tough and so "perfect" in construction that it required more than 900 years of sinning to send their bodies to the grave. Again we quote Pastor Russell:

"The very brief scrap of history furnished us in Genesis, together with the fact that the flood completely obliterated all evidence of the genius and handiwork of the father of our race, and his earliest progeny, give us no basis of calculation respecting his mental and physical abilities. For information we are thrown upon the fact that all God's work is 'perfect,' that man 'sought out many inventions,' and defiled himself *(Ecclesiastes 7:29);* and the fact that even under the curse, and under the unfavorable conditions in which man lived after being thrust out of the Garden of Eden — despite all these unfavorable conditions, so grandly perfect was this human organism, that the father of humanity was sustained for the long period of 930 years, *Genesis 5:5* (*The Atonement,* etc., page 406).

We cannot consistently profess to love the Creator, unless by our work we protect and preserve the home in which He dwells. To love the Creator means the desire to live, the desire to feel the flow of Divine Life, as it surges through our material form; the desire to keep that form in such ideal condition, that the Divine Life will be well pleased to flow through it freely, and abide therein for years and years to come.

When man is moved by such sublime inspirations and impulses, he will search to the utmost ends of the earth to discover and learn the law, and when once he has found it, he will scrupulously follow it.

Has any man so loved the Creator? Did the first man so love his Maker? No. The first man deliberately and absolutely violated the law by polluting his body with the very substance which he knew would cause its destruction. He had so little regard for his well-being, and so little respect for his Maker, that he committed, at the first available opportunity, the crime which he should have shunned with all his strength.

He not only violated the law, but he exhibited his disgusting weakness by endeavoring to shift the responsibility of it to the shoulders of the woman; and she, not to be outdone, promptly laid the burden upon the dumb beast of the field.

And thus was broken the first law, The Great Commandment, the commandment that directed man to respect and reverence the material body, the earthly home of the Divine Life. And man, the Lord of the Visible World, the King of all created things, the spiritual image of the Creator, became a criminal and an outcast, a vagabond and a slave, ruled by the lust of the flesh, with a heart every imagination of the thoughts of which was only evil continually *(Genesis 6:5)*.

# Chapter No. 25
# How Long Should Man Live?

There has been much speculation as to the limit set on the duration of human life. It is written that "his days shall be an hundred and twenty years" *(Genesis 6:3);* and again, that "the days of our years are three-score years and ten; and if by reason of strength they be fourscore years" (Pages 90:10). These statements are based on observation and experience; they are not founded on what should be.

No one knows how long man should live. Science has never dared to set bounds to the possible longevity of human life. No scientist has been bold enough to place a definite limitation on the duration of man's animated existence. The reason is, that all information on this point is most unreliable, being based on past experience; and past experience is that only which has been, and by no means what should have been.

If a man dies at 75, we think he has lived long. That thought is based on experience. If one dies at 110, we are amazed by the information. If another lives 153 years, we are astonished by such length of human life.

Reverting to the Bible, we observe that Nahor dies at 148, while Serug, his father, lived 239 years. Arphaxad dies at 435, while Shem, his father, lived 602 years. And Noah, father of Shem, lived 950 years.

Here is an example of past experience. What does it tell us with reference to the possible or probable length of human life? Nothing. It is merely confusing and perplexing. Why did Nahor die at 148, while Noah, only eight generations removed from Nahor, lived 950 years? How can a limitation be placed on the possible duration of human existence, in the face of such wide and unaccountable variations?

But you are not inclined to believe that Noah lived 950 years, in years that are as long as the years of today. You hold that the age of the old patriarchs was computed in years that are much shorter than those of the present time — not more than one-fourth the period. If this last statement were true, Methuselah would have lived only 243 years, Terah 51, and Abraham 44. Enoch would have been only 16 when he begat Methuselah, Arphaxad less than 9 when he begat Salah, and Salah 7 years old when he begat Eber. Adam would have been more than a great grandfather at 33.

At what period of human existence did the change take place in which time and years are computed? Was it before the Flood? Was it after the Flood? Let us see. According to the Bible, 1656 years elapsed from the birth of Adam to the Flood. Adam lived 930 years, and at his death Methuselah was 243 years old. Noah was 600 years old when Methuselah died; and Shem was 450 when Noah died.

Noah and also Shem come to us from the other world — the world that was before the Flood. Noah was 600 years old when the flood of waters was upon the earth; and he lived after the flood 350 years *(Genesis 7:6; 9:28)*.

Shem, Noah's son, was 100 years old when Methuselah died. He lived to see both Abraham and Isaac, Abraham's son, come into the world. Abraham was 150 years old, and Isaac was 50 years old, when Shem died. In fact, when we recollect that Shem died only 10 short years before the birth of Jacob and Esau, it seems that we can almost reach back in our imagination and touch him, the son of Noah, who was 100 years old when the flood of waters was upon the earth, and who lived after the flood 500 long years.

This stretch of time, from the birth of Adam to the death of Shem, brings us from 1656 years before the Flood to 500 years after the Flood — a total of 2156 years; and still there is no evidence to indicate that any change has occurred in the method of computing time and years. This brings us down so near, in fact, to Noah and Shem that we can almost feel their wonderful presence in our midst. In view of these facts and figures, and the great variation which they indicate in the length of human life, who can say how long man should live?

When we consider the great and wonderful preparation that was made for the advent of man on earth, it is plainly evident that he was constructed and intended to live many years more than he now lives. Covering a period of time so vast that the mind reels in attempting to measure it, the earth, at first a great molten mass, whirling through infinite space, gradually cooled and solidified, and was slowly formed for habitation.

Some say that the materials of which the earth is composed, were at one time in such a superheated state as to be in gaseous form, and that it was whirling through space at terrific speed. Who would dare to attempt to estimate the many thousands of years that passed, while the earth was changing from this state to a condition suitable to sustain living forms? And how many thousands of years more elapsed, from the time that fish appeared in the sea until man appeared on the land?

Following the account recorded in the Bible, which account is sustained by scientific investigation, we observe that living forms first appeared in the water; then fowls that may fly above the earth; then the living creatures after his kind, cattle, and creeping things, and the beasts of the earth; and lastly, man, the marvelous masterpiece of material creation.

Of all forms of animal life, man is much the slowest in reaching maturity. He is the only creature that has a prolonged infancy and childhood. Compare a baby of 12 months with a dog, a cow, or a horse of that age. The human arrives at maturity at 28 to 30 years of age, while the cow reaches that stage in about one-seventh of the time. Shall we believe that there is no deep significance lying back of the slow development of man, and the great amount of time and labor spent in preparing the world for his coming?

The world was slowly prepared through long ages for the advent of man; and he, the last of living forms to appear, is many years in arriving at full maturity from birth. Shall we believe that the Master Builder deliberately pursued this long and carefully planned labor merely that man might come into existence for a few short years, catch a fleeting glimpse of the Glory of his God, and vanish into forgetful nothingness?

Even man, in all his frailty and imperfection, does better than this. Suppose you were planning to erect a magnificent edifice. Of course you would first look well to the foundation, knowing that your building could last no longer than the rock upon which it rested. After you had dug deep down to bed rock, and on it placed your stone foundation, would you be so silly as to build thereon a weak, wooden structure that would topple over under the force of the first brisk wind?

You may think this picture overdrawn, but it is not. It is a fair illustration of what the Master Architect would be guilty of, were He, after all the long planning and preparation that He has made for the coming forth of man, to limit man's animated existence here on earth to a brief period of a few short years.

If experience shows the contrary, it proves nothing. For we shall not believe that man was brought into existence for the few short, sad, and suffering years, such as he now sees, after all the slow, careful, and thorough preparation of the world for his appearance.

# Chapter No. 26
# The Fountain of Youth

Why has man always searched for the fabled "fountain of youth?" Why has he continually believed in the thought that his earthly existence could be prolonged, if he but knew how to prolong it? Why have poets always sung of a time when the pain of disease would be unknown, and the sting of death unfelt?

The last enemy that shall be destroyed is death, wrote Paul *(1 Corinthians 15:26)*. And this thought, the thought that death shall eventually be conquered, instead of being submitted to, is a thought that fills our literature down to the cradle of human history. How could such thoughts be so constant and so persistent, if back of them there did not lie some profound, but as yet an undiscovered principle?

Men do not determine what they shall think. Thoughts are things over which we have little control. We only open our senses, clear away, as we can, all obstruction from the fact, and suffer the mind to see beyond the hoop of our horizon. In every man's mind, thoughts, which appear to come without effort, enter and remain, and afterward, by pondering over them, they illustrate to him certain important laws.

The thought of Eternal Life comes to us without effort. We may struggle against it, and try to drive it away, but it will not down. Every book we read, ever sermon we hear, every lesson we learn, brings to us one thought — Eternal Life. "The immortality of man," says Emerson "is as legitimately preached from the intellections as from the moral volitions."

Life, Divine Life, flowing and surging through our bodies. Who grows weary of its presence? Who is ready to part with it and lay it aside? Ah, not one. Instead of life for a few short years, Eternal Life is the only state that will satisfy man. And to that end is bent all human endeavor. The sole aim of all labor and effort is to find, not life for a few short years, but the Life that has no end.

How could man have thoughts of perpetual youth, if there were no such thing or condition? He sees people dying on all sides — some old and gray, some in the prime of their existence, others in the tender years of childhood. If this state were the regular and natural order of affairs, would or could the thoughts of perpetual youth find lodgment in the mind of man?

And how stupidly do some of the would-be leaders of the race, now and then, treat this the greatest of all human problems; and how illogically do they attempt to explain it away. Says Garrett A. Norton, M. D.:

"When the eccentric and adventurous Spaniard, Ponce de Leon, in 1513, pushed out from shore on poorly charted seas, in search of the mythical fountain of eternal youth, about which liars told marvelous tales, he was reacting to a natural impulse, which is the dread of the infirmities of age and the horror of death" (*Philosophy Of Health,* July, 1926, page 153).

To say that in the "search of the mythical fountain of eternal youth," there is nothing greater lying back of the continual urge, than that of human "reaction to a natural impulse, which is the dread of the infirmities of age and the horror of death," is to dismiss the matter in a superficial manner, that falls far short of a satisfactory explanation.

Did the Grand Architect labor long and carefully, for no other purpose than to bring man into existence for a few short years, and torture and torment him all his days with "the dread of the infirmities of age and the horror of death?" If that view of the problem is the correct one, then we can with propriety ask, why did the Creator make man at all?

From the standpoint of reason, it seems that it would be a strange God who, knowing the end from the beginning, would construct matter into the form of man, animate that form with His Spirit, allow that form to roam the earth for a few short years, and fill those years with "the dread of the infirmities of age and the horror of death."

The view, to most people, may be so completely satisfying as to leave nothing more to be desired; but to us it is entirely meaningless, and is only the babble and twaddle of the outside man, expressing in its perfection all its physical limitations.

# Chapter No. 27
# Was Man Born To Die?

Why does man die? Why is it that some persons die at the young age of 20, or even sooner, while others live 100 years, and sometimes longer?

The daily press of February 21, 1927, states that in carrying out the 1927 census in Russia, government inspector's discovered nearly 150 persons in scattered parts of the country, who are more than 100 years old. The most notable case is that of Ivan Shapkovsky, a hardy mountaineer, whose birth certificate showed that he was born six years after the American Declaration of Independence, making him 145 years old.

Among the oldest women is Mariana Maliarevitch, who came into the world 131 years ago, just as Catherine the Great was passing out. She walked 20 miles in the snow to the census office, to make sure that the officials would not fail to register her among the country's 140,000,000 other inhabitants.

Zora Agha, of Turkey, is reported by the press of April 2, 1927, as being alive at the age of 153 years, and never ill until a few years ago, when he was taken to Italy to be exhibited. In the press of April 24, 1926, we learned that one Doctor Lee Masten Francis, 50 years old, a widely known physician of Buffalo, N. Y., died suddenly at a medical convention in Dallas, Texas shortly after reading a "scientific paper" before the body of physicians. The press reported that —

"Doctor Francis had apparently been in good health, his friends said, though some of them feared that he may have been suffering from athletic heart."

Zora Agha is an illiterate Turk, and is said to have worked all his life at the most menial, servile labor. Doctor Francis would have regarded him as the lowest type of an ignoramus. But what benefit did Doctor Francis derive from his highly-prized medical education? Here is an example that startlingly reveals the worthlessness of medical education and progression, of which civilization so proudly boasts. Men are far better off without it, as shown by the average short life-span of medical men. Savage tribes are to be envied for their freedom from the withering medical curse that is corrupting and degenerating civilized nations.

If Life will operate through the body of Zora Agha for 153 years, why did it cease to operate through the body of Doctor Francis at the end of 50 years? If Life operates through one material body only 20 years, why does it operate through another eight times that long? And if it will operate through another body eight times 20 years, why should it not continue so to operate for 10, 20, or 50 times 20 years? What happens to stop the operation of Life? We would be wrong in assuming that it stops without good and sufficient cause.

When we study the matter but superficially, we immediately perceive, from the wide variation of the length of human life, that something is wrong. There appears to be no definite limitation that rules in this department of human existence, For, in that event, each man, barring accidents, would live a certain length of time and die at a certain age.

The Universe is governed by law, and this department of existence is not beyond the influence of law. Nor do we believe that the Law-giver ever decrees, without good and sufficient cause, that the son of a multi-millionaire shall die at 20, while the son of a beggar shall live 150 years. There is a cause back of everything that occurs, and that cause is and must always be the efficient and sufficient equal of all that follows.

If a man in this day and time lives 100 years, it is considered a remarkable feat; and when men die at 75, we feel that they have lived to a "ripe old age." This is because we know no better. We judge by experience; and experience, no matter how erroneous it may be when compared with facts, always closes our understanding to what should have been.

The eagle lives 500 years; some species of parrots live 600 to 700 years; the tortoise lives 1000 years; the whale lives 1500 years; and the alligator lives 1800 years. The lowly swine, conspicuous in its domesticated state for ill-health and short life, in its wild state lives free from disease to the age of 300 years.

But man, the lord of the visible realm, the only creature possessed of reason and judgment, with intelligence to determine the effect on his body of the influence of a favorable or an unfavorable environment, with power to make such changes in his environment as may be conducive to his health and welfare knows so little about how to live, that he dies of "old age" at 75.

"Was man born to die like the beasts?" asks Pastor Russell. He remarks:

"What was the purpose of God respecting man in his creation? We see that so far as the brute creation is concerned, the Lord's evident design was that they should live a few years and then die, giving place to others of the species; and that thus they should minister as servants to the pleasure and convenience of man, their master, who in his perfection was a gracious master.

"But how about man? Was man born to die like the beast? We have just seen that he had no undying quality bestowed upon him, but we find abundant testimony of God's provision for the everlasting life of all who attained to approved conditions" (*The Atonement,* etc., page 399).

Man may not have been born "to die like the beasts," but by his shameful mistreatment of his body he has fallen far below the dumb brute, so far as his physical existence is concerned. Of this Charles Newman Curtis states:

"How far man has fallen through disobedience from his high natural position. The darkening of his reason, the blinding of his spiritual sight, the blunting of his conscience, the distraction of his mind, and the disorder and disease of his body — how appalling! The history of religions reveals this woeful blight" (*An Epoch In The Spiritual Life*, page 301).

Man was created mortal — in a condition in which death was a possibility, or everlasting life a possibility, depending upon his conduct, whether he obeyed or disobeyed the law. "Had he remained obedient," says Pastor Russell, "he would have continued living until now — and forever — and, yet all the while he would have been mortal, liable to death if disobedient." Russell continues:

"We find abundant testimony of God's provision for the everlasting life (in the flesh) of all who attained to approved conditions."

Drummond observes:

"One of the most startling achievements of recent science is a definition of Eternal Life. To the religious mind this is a contribution of immense moment. For 1800 years only one definition of Eternal Life was before the world. Now there are two."

What arc the two definitions? Drummond gives them as follows:

(1) This is Life Eternal — that they might know Thee, the True God, and Jesus Christ whom Thou hast sent — Jesus Christ.

(2) Perfect correspondence would be perfect life. Were there no changes in the environment but such as the organism had adapted changes to meet, and were it never to fail in the efficiency with which it met them, there would be eternal existence and eternal knowledge. — *Herbert Spencer*.

The first definition relates to Spiritual Life; the second explains how eternal life in the flesh is possible by a supplement of proper conditions. Of Spencer's observations Drummond says:

"He is analyzing with minute care the relations between Environment and Life. He unfolds the principle according to which Life is high or low, long or short. He shows why organisms live and why they die. And finally he defines a condition of things in which an organism would never die — in which it would enjoy a perpetual and perfect life."

Drummond then shows that man, by means of his more complex organism, is more completely equipped with "adapted changes" than any other animal, to meet and master, or control we had better say, his Environment. He observes:

"The organism then with the most perfect set of correspondences, that is, the highest and most complex organism, has an obvious advantage over less complex forms. It can adjust itself more perfectly and frequently. But this is just the biological way of saying that it can live the longest. And hence the relation between complexity and longevity may be expressed thus — the most complex organisms are the longest lived."

We are beginning to recognize the Voice of the Soul. We are beginning to understand the why of the continual urge in man to search for the Fountain Of Youth. We observe that this influence has back of it more than the dream of a diseased mind, or the fancy of an "eccentric and adventurous Spaniard."

Man dies, not because of his age, not because it is impossible for him to live longer, but because, through defiance of the law, he forfeits his right and privilege to live longer. In other words, a man lives only so long as he knows how to live, and he dies because of his lack of knowledge of how to live longer. To explain in detail why a man dies, or how he should live, in order to maintain his body in such perfect condition that Life would inhabit it forever, as it does for a certain period of time, is a subject too large for the scope of this work. The reader will find much information on this question in our book, *The Law of Life and Human Health*, (available at www.frontlinebookpublishing.com) the teaching of which will benefit him greatly.

All that we hope to show in this limited space is, that the deep and persistent thought of perpetual youth, which has come down to us from the earliest times, really has back of it a truth which, until now, has never been explored and investigated. It is this truth that has continuously welled up in man's heart, and urged him on and on, in his ceaseless search of ways and means to defeat death, and acquire that which men crave above all other things — perpetual youth.

If we are to take Moses by what he says, he indicates that he believed in the immortality of the flesh; and he bases his opinion as to the cause of the destruction of the body on the fact, that the law was violated in not supplying the body with suitable nourishment. And death was the logical result of this transgression.

So long as man ate "of the fruit of the trees of the garden," the perfect food, his body could not decay, since its requirements for building material were fully met. But when man was driven from the garden, and compelled to "eat the herb of the field," his body immediately began to deteriorate. For the imperfect "herb of the field" could not be substituted for "the fruit of the trees," as food for the body, and sustain it in perfect health.

The human body was made to subsist on fruits, the highest and most perfect food in Nature. When something else was substituted, the needs of the body were not supplied, and its dissolution became only a matter of time, just as a river would dry up and come to an end, if it were fed with saw-dust or sand instead of with water.

If man had been born to die, death would be a natural sequence or condition, just as living, sleeping, eating, drinking, working, etc., and man would harbor no more "dread of the infirmities of age and the horror of death," than he does of living from day to day, or of growing sleepy, hungry, thirsty, or tired. A normal man does not dread these natural conditions. He enjoys them. He finds pleasure in growing drowsy and hungry and thirsty, for he experiences joy in gratifying these desires. What a sad state, if we were compelled to gaze upon the ripe, golden, luscious fruit, yet lack the hunger that gives us pleasure to eat of it.

If to die were a natural condition, the natural end of man, then to die would be as pleasant as to live, or eat, or sleep; for no decrees of the Law-giver carries "dread and horror" to any but to law violators, and they alone are the criminals that must suffer. So far, the law violators have included all men from the beginning, for not one single individual has obeyed the law.

It is the unnatural state that engenders the unnatural feeling. It is because man was not made to die, that he looks upon death with "horror." Eminent physiologists, men standing at the very top of their profession, have said that, according to their findings, it is less difficult to explain why man does not live forever, than to explain why he dies.

Professor Weismann observes:

"Death is not a primitive attribute of living matter; it is of secondary origin. There are animals that never die; for instance, the infusorians and rhizopods, and, in general, all unicellular organisms."

Doctor Munroe states:

"The human frame as a machine is perfect; that it contains within itself no marks by which we can possibly predict its decay; it is apparently intended to go on forever."

Doctor B. Stanford Claunch remarks:

"The living organism is potentially immortal. There is no physiological nor biological reason for death. But we are born into a world of error — of physical and mental limitations. No sooner do we come into being, than these limitations and conditions, detrimental to eternal living existence, are thrust upon us."

Seneca, the Roman philosopher, is reported to have once said:

*"People do not die, they kill themselves."*

We shall see that this is literally so, for we shall show that regardless of the number of times the Sun rises and sets, man's body is never more than seven years old, and some hold that this may be reduced to one year. And to end the existence of such a marvelous organism, one would have to kill it. That is exactly what a man does — he actually commits suicide by a slow gradual, but positive process.

# Chapter No. 28
## Influence of Suggestion

Ask in (spiritual) prayer, believing, ye shall receive *(Matthew 21:22)*. I have not found so great faith, no, not in Israel *(Matthew 8:10)*. Go thy way; and as thou hast believed, so be it done unto thee *(Matthew 8:13)*.

Man believes from the day that he is old enough to think and reason, that he must die; and as a man thinketh in his heart, so is he. The Master Psychologist knew to what extent the Mind controls the body, and He was always careful to arouse favorable mental conditions in those who sought His help.

Adam violated the first law given to man, and through the influence of suggestion poisoned his mind with the fear of the punishment that had been prescribed. His guilty conscience sorely troubled him; and he hid himself in the depth of the forest, and trembled with fear at each unusual sound of the wind blowing through the tree-tops. All sorts of weird imaginations rose up in his mind, and he thought he could hear the angry voice of the Creator "walking in the garden." He imagined that the voice was calling to him, saying, "Where art thou?"

Adam was a dead man from that moment. For the organs of the body are keenly responsive to thought. Who has not seen the face redden with rage, or whiten with fear? These external expressions are indications of abnormal function occurring within the body as the result of abnormal mental states. The mental states of fear, worry, anger, jealousy, etc., construct poisons within the system by affecting the function of its organs. These poisons destroy the body and produce death, just as we have been told — Wherefore, as by one man sin entered into the world, and death by sin; and so death passed upon all men *(Romans 5:12)*. Every man is tempted, when he is drawn away of his own lust, and enticed. Then when lust hath conceived, it bringeth forth sin: and sin, when it is finished, bringeth forth death *(James 1:14, 15)*.

By his becoming a criminal at the outset, man's own guilty conscience condemned him to death, in accordance with the law as it was decreed. So down through the ages, the thought has been continually engendered in the heart of every man, that he is born to die, and he makes no systematic effort to conquer death by discovering the law that rules his being, then living strictly in accordance with that law.

"We are born into a world of error — of physical and mental limitations. No sooner do we come into being, than these limitations and conditions, detrimental to eternal living existence, are thrust upon us," says Doctor Claunch. And no man tries to dodge the thrust.

On the other hand, the still, small voice continues to whisper into the ear of every man, that he should not die; and between these powerful, opposing influences, man is more helpless than child.

A secret and persistent urge, which he does not fully understand because of past experience, tells man that he should never grow old, much less die; and this is confirmed as a fact by the findings of anatomists, physiologists and biologists. But experience has shown him that all men so far have died from the first; and from this he erroneously concludes that there is for him no escape from death. So he resigns himself to what he regards as the inevitable. To what extent the Mind influences the body; no one is able to say. But there are many examples in history to indicate that, through the influence of suggestion, the mind is capable of setting up processes of function that are either detrimental or beneficial, depending on the character of suggestion in a given case. Of this Doctor Hereward Carrington makes the following remarks:

"There are numerous cases on record where continued contemplation of, and dwelling upon the scene of the crucifixion have resulted in the appearance of bleeding spots or patches in the skin, corresponding, in their location, to the wounds of Christ. This was first recorded in the case of Francis of Assisi; and there have been numerous other cases — one of the best known and most recent being that of Louise Lateau, near Mons, France, which was much discussed in 1868" (*Vitality, Fasting & Nutrition,* page 427).

Doctor Moll, in discussing the above case, observes:

"It appears from the literature concerning her, that the anatomical process was rather a complicated one in her case. Blisters first appeared, and after they burst, there was bleeding from the true skin (corium), without any visible injury. Lateau directed her own attention continually to those parts of her body which, she knew, corresponded to the wounds of Christ, and the anatomical lesions resulted from this strain of attention, as in other cases from external suggestion. In the well-known case of Catherine Emeriti, the bleedings are said to have appeared while she was looking at the crucifix,"

Doctor Rybilkin, in the presence of his colleagues, at the hospital Marie, in St. Petersburg, performed the following experiment on a young man 16 years old, whom the doctor hypnotized, and then suggested to him that:

"When you awake, you will be cold; you will go and warm yourself at the stove, and you will burn your forearm on the line which I have traced out. This will hurt you; redness will appear on your arm: it will swell; there will be blisters.

"On being awakened, the patient obeyed the suggestion. He even uttered a cry of pain at the moment when he touched the door of the stove, which of course was cold. Some minutes later a redness, without swelling, could be seen at the place indicated; and the patient complained of sharp pain on its being touched. A bandage was put on his arm, and he went to bed under our eyes. When the dressing was removed at ten next morning we saw at the place of the burn two blisters, one the size of a nut, the other of a pea, and a number of small blisters. Around this tract the skin was red and sensitive."

The same powerful influence that will produce wounds on the body, will not only help to induce the approach of age, but will also serve to hold age at bay. This fact is often mentioned in history, and one particular case in mind, is that of an English lady, who, according to the London Lancet, a medical magazine, being disappointed in love in early life, became insane. Unconscious of the fleeting years, she still lived in the hour that had parted her lover and her, and she arose and carefully arranged her toilet each day, and watched through the window for the one that was never to come.

Days passed into months, and months into years; but she knew it not. To her there was no such thing as time. Her mind still lingered and lived in that youthful day, and her youthful appearance remained unchanged. At the age of 74 she seemed to be no more than 20. There were no gray hairs, no wrinkled brow, no dimming of the eye, no lessening of vitality, no signs of decay. The coming and going of the years had not affected her body, because it had not affected her mind. To that particular phase of existence, her mind was blank.

It is only in recent years that the potency and the extent of the influence of the mind over the body is beginning to be recognized. And this influence can be directed into constructive channels as well as destructive ones. If fear, worry, sorrow, suffering, hate, anger, etc., are mental states that have destructive tendencies on the body, then faith, hope, happiness, love, cheer, and so on, are mental states that have constructive tendencies on the body. It is through these constructive mental states that good results are obtained by divine healers, spiritual healers, mental healers, hypnotic healers, Christian science healers, medical healers, and all healers.

The same influence that produces destructive tendencies, will, on a reversal of the lever, also produce constructive tendencies. The same faith that removes the mountain from the path will also place the mountain in our path. By a process of constant adverse suggestion, extending through the entire genealogy of the race, man builds into his blood, tissues, bones, and even into the mind, the destructive thought that gradually degenerates his frame, and finally helps to destroy it. By constant adverse suggestion, he so interferes with the normal function of the body, that it develops into an abnormal, distorted condition, and Life is unable to control the form through which it operates, and so departs because it can remain no longer.

Thus man murders himself.

To what heights could man rise, if he but conquered his perverted habits and his mental state. The mental state of fear alone is responsible for much damage resulting to the body. Fear makes men slaves. Fear makes the face pallid, retards or quickens the heartbeat, changes the nature of the body's secretions, and alters the body's function in all respects. Fear puts wrinkles in the face, turns the hair white, and brings men to the grave. The Bible, from beginning to end, contains one continuous admonition to cast fear out of the heart.

We must cast out fear, we must reform our mental state, we must have faith. But the reader is cautioned against falling into the error of feeling, that any amount of persuasion can coerce us into believing that the influence of suggestion and faith can overcome the influence of the law, and conquer the degenerating effect on the body, that arises from such maltreatment as the nourishing of it on soft lead, and the giving to it of water to drink that contains fine sand, in order to still and satisfy its call for material to repair, replace, and renew its worn and wasted parts.

# Chapter No. 29
# Conditions of Eternal Life

What is eternal Life? Christ defined it spiritually; Herbert Spencer defined it materially. For 1800 years but one definition of eternal life was before the world. Thru all these ages religion had this doctrine to itself. But now modern biology has given us a definition of eternal life in the flesh, based on an accurate examination of the necessary conditions. Why a subject so vital as the latter definition has lain unnoticed all these years, and received no attention, is difficult to understand.

According to these two definitions, eternal life is possible both in the spirit and in the flesh. How startling that last statement must sound to those who know nothing of the principle underlying the function of the human organism.

Let us analyze the subject somewhat briefly: I die daily, said Paul *(1 Corinthians 15:31)*. That statement is literally true, so far as the body is concerned. Every man's body is dying daily, hourly; part of a man's body dies every second. Time has no effect on the age of the body. This we have seen.

All the effect that time has on the body comes through the influence of the mind. Keeps the mind thinking proper thoughts give the body the building material and the care it needs, then, so far as age and time are concerned, blank the mind entirely, and perpetual youth is a reality, not a dream.

Since this declaration is so contrary to all experience, more light is required to give it force. We shall give it by comparing the body to a man-made machine — a procedure that medical men delight in performing, yet in the performance of which they neglect the most important part, as we shall see. If a machine is incapable of being worn out, it is for that reason incapable of coming to an end, without some accident occurring. We shall see that the body is incapable of being worn out, with proper care, and should, barring accidents, never come to an end.

Let us compare the living organism to a stationary steam engine, carefully constructed of the finest steel, mechanically perfect, operating smoothly, all parts working in harmony with one another. Now let us elevate the engine to the high plane of the living body, by giving it the same powers which the body possesses. Let us equip it with the same inherent, automatic, and practically unlimited powers of self-starting, self-building,      self-operating, self-adjusting, self-repairing, self-renovating, self-renewing, and self-governing.

Under these circumstances, no man could do to or for that engine, but supply it with the material it needed, of the kind needed, at the time needed, and in the quantity needed, for its use, repair, renewal, reconstruction, etc., and that engine, at the end of ten thousand years, or ten million years, would be the same, running the same, performing the same, and be in the same condition in every detail, as during the first year of its existence. It would be as impossible for such a machine to grow old, wear out, decay, and fall to ruin, as for the Sun to rise in the West.

The engine, no less than the human body, is governed by a certain law. The life of the engine would soon come to an end, if that law were not known, observed, and obeyed. For instance, if we feed the engine soft lead, instead of finely tempered steel, for use in repairing its wear and tear; and, in place of high-grade oil, used water containing fine sand to "lubricate" its bearings and joints, what would happen? We know without experience that such mal-treatment would soon derange its smooth operation, weaken its structure, grind out its parts, and start it rapidly on the road to ruin. Its life would come to an end just as quickly as such mal-treatment had time to bring about its down-fall and destruction.

The living body is perfectly equipped with inherent, automatic, and practically unlimited powers of self-starting, self-building, self-operating, self-adjusting, self-repairing, self-renovating, self-regenerating, self-renewing, and self-governing. No man can do more for the body than supply it with the material it needs, of the quantity and quality it needs, at the time it needs it, and use the body as it was intended to be used. More than this the body does not require, and more than this the body cannot receive. Under such ideal conditions, there is no more reason for the body's wearing out, decaying and falling to ruin, than for the engine to do so.

This is just another way of stating Spencer's definition of eternal living existence. "Were there no changes in the environment but such as the organism had adapted changes to meet, and were it never to fail in the efficiency with which it met them, there would be eternal (living) existence."

There is nothing in the condition prescribed by Spencer that is lacking, so far as the organism and its environment are concerned. The human body, in the beginning, if not now, was constructed perfect; and it was then, if not now, in an environment, the changes of which the organism was equipped with adapted changes to meet; and it would never have failed in the efficiency with which it met the changes, but for the interference of man.

# Chapter No. 30
# How Old is the Body?

We have seen that the body, under the operation of Divine Life, is undergoing a constant process of destruction and construction. It is formed by the multiplication and differentiation of millions of tiny cells. The cells increase in number by the division of the pre-existing cells into equal parts, and each part possesses similar properties. Every new cell has a definite life-history. It grows, performs its function, and ceases to exist, either by dividing into two other cells, or by dying, dissolving, and passing from the body as waste.

While the multiplication rate exceeds the death rate of cells in any certain tissue or organ, that tissue or organ increases in size. When the multiplication-rate and the death-rate are equal, the tissue or organ is in a state of equilibrium. As soon as the death-rate exceeds the multiplication-rate, decay and atrophy begin; and when the decay and atrophy have proceeded to such an extent that an important tissue or organ can no longer perform its allotted function, the animated existence of the body comes to an end — the body dies.

General decay and death, therefore, are the logical result of the loss of multiplication power of the cells of the body. This loss of power of the cells to perform their function result from the fact, that the law which governs the body is not being observed and obeyed. We should know without experience that the needs of the body, as the needs of the engine, are not being fully supplied or that the body is being misused and abused.

As we observe, there is a continuous change going on in the entire structure of the body, by which its various parts are constantly broken down and cast off as unfit for further use, and as constantly renewed. Throughout the whole body, the Life Force is incessantly engaged in tearing down the old tissues, of which the body is composed, and in rebuilding them again of new, fresh materials; so that all the tissues and parts of the body are always renewed and always ready to perform their allotted function.

Doctor Carrington comments on the renewal process occurring in the body as follows:

"The moment the last morsel of food is digested, and the stomach is empty, a general reconstructive process begins; a new tissue formation, owing to the fact that the broken-down cells are being replaced by (new) healthy ones — which is *Nature's* method of repairing any destroyed or injured part of the organism. This replacement of cells means gradual replacement of tissues; replacement of tissues means that a new stomach has been constructed—a stomach in every sense of the word NEW — as new in every anatomical sense as is the filling in of wounds, or between the fractured ends of bones" (*Vitality, Fasting, Nutrition,* page 490).

All the cells composing the soft tissues are thus completely renewed in a few months. Anatomists and physiologists are not agreed among themselves as to the length of time required to renew all the bony structures; but seven years is the maximum estimate. Doctor Carrington thinks this time limit too long. He says:

"Now, since the present modes of living are monstrously abnormal; and since our bodies are, consequently, distinctly abnormal in composition and function throughout our lives, it follows that all such changes will be abnormal also, and that the length of time occupied in all such changes is, at the present day, and under existing conditions, entirely abnormal" (*Vitality, Fasting & Nutrition*, page 49I).

"It is my contention that, were cell changes not stunted and at times almost checked by the almost entire monopoly of the vital forces for the purposes of digestion and elimination, is could be definitely ascertained that the body changes with the seasons, as does the snake's skin; and I look for the not far distant day when science shall prove this to be a fact — by the observation of normal men and women, instead of diseased ones — the method now in vogue" (*Supra,* page 492).

However, taking the maximum estimate as given, regardless of how long a man lives, HIS BODY IS NEVER MORE THAN SEVEN YEARS OLD. Why then does the body grow stiff, feeble, and decay? For the same reason that a mighty river would cease to exist, or an engine would grow defective and fall to ruin — because its constant needs are not completely and properly met. When we violate the law by which a thing is, then and there its dissolution begins. It may be a river, a machine, or a man, but the result is the same. When there occurs a violation of the law by which a river, machine, or man is, its end is but a question of time.

More light is shed on the subject by the experience of Doctor Alexis Carrel, as related by Doctor Shelton, to-wit:

"On January 17, 1912, Doctor Carrel tack a piece of connective tissue from the heart of a chicken and set about to maintain its life apart from the chicken's body. That piece of heart is alive yet (1926), and is, apparently, as strong and vigorous as ever. Every day it is washed and supplied with a fresh nutrient media. The washing completely rids it of waste products. Kept clean and properly nourished, it grows so rapidly that it is frequently necessary to subdivide it. Yet the piece of heart does not seem to grow old in the sense that its vitality is diminished. On November 21, 1925, it was announced that so rapid had been the growth of this piece of tissue, that had it not been cut down each day, it would have overspread the entire city of New York" (*Living Life To Live It Longer,* page 13).

Doctor W. R. C. Latson, discussing Harry Gaze's physical immortality theory, says:

"Doctor Gaze advances the somewhat startling claim that somatic death, that is, the death of the body as a whole, is due to causes which may be averted; and that by proper means one may so control the bodily functions as to retain the body indefinitely. I do not hesitate to say that, while his conception of life and the possibility of physical immortality is unique, there is nothing in the accepted facts of physiological science, by which his position can be refuted."

Gaze himself observes:

"The body literally and completely returns to dust in less than one year; and during that period a new body is constructed, molecule by molecule. The question may, therefore, be asked, why does the body ever manifest age if is thus renewed? With the advance of years, there is a gradual but positive cessation of the vitality expressed, resulting from the failure (of the person) to co-operate with the process of renewal."

Linn A. E. Gale remarks:

"Science agrees that death can be deferred and life extended far beyond the prevailing limit. Some scientists go far beyond that, and assert that disease and age will eventually be eradicated to such an extent that death will be the exception" (*Health Messenger*, page 20).

But how will this come about? By casting science and all its junk into the sea, and following Nature. It will come about by correcting our habits, by knowing, observing, and obeying the law. Some light on this point is also given by Doctor Shelton in the following remarks:

"A few years ago Professor Huxley of England, son of the older Professor Huxley, took some young planarian, or earth worms, and performed a very interesting and instructive experiment with them. He fed a whole family of these as they ordinarily eat. One he isolated and fed in the same manner, except that he forced it to undergo short periods of fasting. It was alternately fed and fasted.

"The isolated worm was still alive after 19 generations of its brothers had been born, lived their regular lift cycles, and passed away. The only difference in the mode of life and the diet of this worm, as compared to that of its brother worms, was its periodic fasts.

"Professor Huxley explained that overfeeding clogs the body and produces death. By fasting the worm at repeated intervals, the excess of food that was clogging and poisoning the body, was used up and the toxins or acids were cleared out. The cells and tissues of the worm were kept soft and young and its system kept free from all encumbrances. The result was that it lived over 19 times as long as it otherwise would have lived" *(Supra)*.

If we apply this rule to man, an individual dying at 50 could increase his days to 950 years, and one dying at 100 should live to be 1900 years old. What is possible for worms should be possible for man; for shall we believe that worms are more greatly endowed than man is?

It seems safe to assume that under proper care, the body should not grow feeble and decay under a thousand years. For if man lived perfect in all his habits, no cell of his body would fail to perform its allotted function, and human life, barring accident, would continue for many centuries. Perpetual youth would be a reality instead of a wish, and "the dread of the infirmities of age and the horror of death" would be unknown.

With this fact before us, we are better able to account for the untiring search of man for the "fountain of youth." Back of this urge is an uncanny reality that has never before been clearly described; and it is this reality that has supplied the propelling power which has urged man on and on, in his ceaseless effort to conquer death and escape "old age," by regaining the priceless treasure that he forfeited by disobeying the law *(Genesis 2:17)*.

# Chapter No. 31
# The Human Intellect

The duration of man's physical existence is not determined by, nor limited to, a certain number of years, it seems; nor is his vitality measured and decreased by the rising and setting of the sun.

Youth and age are conditions only, appertaining to the body, but not to Life. For a man is young or old, depending on his physical condition, and not on the force animating his frame. It is not Life that grows old with toil and time; and if the body, through which Life functions, remained forever in a condition favorable for its continuous and harmonious operation, Life would never depart there from.

Give, and it shall be given unto you, is the law *(Luke 6:38)*. Give to your body the scrupulous care that merits eternal life in the flesh, and, since belief produces the effect of belief, also firmly believe that your desire is possible of fulfillment *(Mark 11:24)*, and you shall receive it *(Matthew 7:7)*. The disposition of men to give up and let go when they begin to approach the 60th or 70th mile stone, is the disposition that engenders in their tissues the processes that produce the condition which they visualize in their mind. It is dangerous; cast it from you.

But, say you, all things are "born to die," and all things do die. All vegetal and animal life dies. Why should man alone be excluded from this category?

Why do ye doubt, O ye of little faith *(Matthew 8:26)*. Have you forgotten that there are many reasons why man should not be included in this class? Let us observe some of them: Man is the crowning work of Creation. He is Lord of the Visible Realm, with dominion over every living thing that moveth upon the earth *(Genesis 1:28)*. He alone of all that inhabit the earth, possesses the divine power to think, reason, and understand, by virtue of which he is able to search the ends of the earth, discover and appropriate to his use, the deepest secrets of Nature.

Through the use of his intellect, man alone can detect the existence of Universal Law, can discover the mode and manner of its operation, can change and control his environment to his advantage; can so regulate his conduct as to remain in harmony with the law, and by these means can supply conditions that will inure to his improvement and advancement, just as surely as water flows downward.

Why do we forget these divine attributes, and make so little use of them? Because of ignorance and miss-education. What could man accomplish, were he educated to know the law, put his body in harmony therewith by conquering his perverse nature and habits, and regain the "dominion" that was intended should be his? He would then enjoy the great treasures about which he will know nothing until he rises to that plane.

Man takes a piece of chicken tissue, and supplies a condition that carries its life on and on, in a state of "perpetual youth." By knowing the law and supplying the proper conditions, he should be able to carry the existence of his own body on and on, in a state of "perpetual youth." Why not? If this state is possible for a piece of chicken tissue, it is possible for the whole chicken; and if it is possible for a chicken, it is also possible for a man. Let us notice this briefly:

In the tree we have a symbol of eternal living existence. Some trees survive for several centuries. But in time even the tree, like all other animated forms, decays and dies. This is due to a certain condition which has resulted and which the tree lacks power to control.

The body of a tree, like the body of a man who knows nothing of the law that enables him to rule his environment and retain his vitality, enters into a state of calcification and hardening, due to an accumulation of excess minerals in its trunk, and it is unable to draw adequate nourishment up from its roots through the long stretch of hardened, mineral-ladened wood. So the tree dies of starvation, not from lack of food within reach of its roots, but from lack of ability to absorb and assimilate the food.

But the branches of the tree are still young and vigorous; and if newly rooted, or engrafted onto younger trunks, they will take on renewed vitality, and continue to grow until the state of calcification again threatens their existence. By repeating the process as often as may be necessary, the life of the branches may be prolonged for thousands of years, and they will maintain a state of "perpetual youth."

By virtue of a peculiar intelligence, bestowed upon no other creature, man is able to control the environment of trees, worms, and chicken tissue, and supply conditions that endow these with "perpetual youth." Knowing these things by experience demonstration, why does he not use this information to the benefit of his own body? There appears to be no reason why he should not be able to do for himself what he is able to do for trees, worms, and chicken tissue.

There are many who will sneer at these remarks, as their forefathers sneered at the thought of wireless telegraphy, horseless carriages, and flying machines. But sneering did not prevent these things from coming to pass. Man can control his own environment as well as that of worms and trees. By the acquisition and application of knowledge of how to live as he should live, man can prevent the calcification and hardening of his blood vessels, tissues, organs, and joints, and thus gain for himself the "perpetual youth" which has always been the dream of the race.

For instance, if a man observes by his feelings that he is losing his vitality, he is able to restore it again, just as he does for trees and worms, by so living as to regenerate and rejuvenate his body. This is done we see, first by fasting until the body has dissolved and disposed of the hardening deposits; then by eating sparingly of such foods, and drinking only such liquids, as will leave in his body no hardening deposits, and observe the other requirements for health, such as sleeping, right-thinking, exercising, bathing, etc.

Here lies part of the secret; and these things man alone can learn and do. So far, no man has learned and done them to a degree of perfection. Still, "an event which has not yet taken place, is as much a part of universal truth as though it had occurred." And because it has not yet come to pass, is no proof that such event is impossible. Man knows those things only that has happened, and believes as impossible events that have not happened; but that does not make it so. For all things are possible to him that believeth (and doeth) *(Mark 9:23)*.

We are especially cautioned not to depend on faith to the exclusion of work. To accomplish what is desired in any department of human existence requires work. It requires not only faith, but work. It requires work — a doing of that which we believe, that what we desire may come to pass. It is written:

"What doth it profit, my brethren, though a man say he hath faith, and have not works? Can faith save him? But wilt thou know, o vain man, that faith without works is dead" *(James 2:14-20)*.

Now and then we read of someone who has made a little more than the ordinary use of the powers which obey the beck and call of man, and are astonished by the remarkable results that are accomplished. Louis Cornaro makes but partial use of them, and from a physical wreck at the age of 40, given up by physicians as hopeless, he brings himself back from the shadows of death, to a state of health and vigor that carries him onward through life to the age of 102 years — and he lived to see planted every one of the physicians who solemnly assured him that he could live but a few short years. This is only one of multitudes of similar cases.

Now if Cornaro, by his ability to control his environment, was able to supply conditions sufficiently favorable to bring him back from the brink of the grave at the age of 40, to a degree of health that enabled him to live 62 years longer, why could he not have supplied conditions so favorable as to enable him to live 602 or 6002 or 60002 years longer? He could, and he would have done so, had he known how. It is a matter of knowing how.

No man has yet died a natural death, this statement applies to all men who have appeared on earth from the first, including Methuselah, who is said to have lived almost a thousand years — for death is not natural. If a man can live 100 years, he can live 1000 years, and if he can live 1000 years, there is no reason. Why he should die.

We make this statement, since no man ever died because Life was ready and willing to leave his body. Life is endowed with unlimited power and unlimited resource; and it strives persistently to save and preserve the form through which it operates, without varying in the least from its course. Let us see.

The muscles grow soft and flabby and weak from non-use; but indulge in vigorous exercise for a few weeks, and observe how quickly Life increases their size and endurance, in order to meet the new demand made upon them. The skin on the palm of the hands grows thin and tender through lack of labor, and the hands soon blister and pain when we use them in hard work. What happens? Continue the work and see how soon Life provides there, skin of extra thickness and toughness, to meet the new demands. This illustrates the operation of the law, Give, and it shall be given unto you; good measure, pressed down, and shaken together, and running over *(Luke 6:38)*.

These two examples are typical of the marvelous manner in which Life always strives, under the influence of the Law of Self-preservation, to protect and preserve as long as possible, its mundane habitation. Every part of the body responds to this law, no matter whether it be the skin, the muscles, or the internal organs. It may be the heart, the liver, kidneys, or ductless glands; but since they are all a part of the whole, they respond to the law that governs the whole.

When the function of Life is obstructed in the smallest degree, it promptly rises to meet and master the situation, as we have shown, for the purpose of preserving the body it has brought into existence. In cases of severe illness, we know that Life often succeeds in saving the body after all human hope is lost. But if, due to the interference of man, the obstruction is too great for it to conquer, then it must depart from the body, and the body sinks back into the earth, not because it could not live longer, but because, through the disobedience of its owner, it has forfeited its right to live longer.

# Chapter No. 32
# From Master to Slave

No creature of the animal kingdom, save and except man, dies prematurely of pestilence and disease, when left in its native state. This is so because they live in peace and harmony with their environment.

Having no will of their own, the animals of the wild are guided by an unerring intelligence that is uncanny when contemplated, and are constrained to live in obedience to the law of their being. These intelligence men call Animal Instinct, and so little is known of it that we have discussed the same in a separate chapter.

A noteworthy fact that comes up in connection with the recorded existence of the old Patriarchs is the conspicuous absence of information or evidence to indicate that these men were ever ill, or died prematurely. They passed thru their earthly sojourn, from birth to death, like vigorous oaks that grow on suitable soil under ideal conditions.

There is only one recorded exception, and that is in the case of Enoch, father of Methuselah. All the days of Enoch were 365, and Enoch walked with God, and he was not; for God took him *(Genesis 5:22-24)*.

But contemplate man of today: The highest and noblest of all living creatures, the only beings capable of reason and judgment, and possessed with powers of intelligence for carrying into execution such arts and designs as science and philosophy may discover and dictate — this man comes not so near, by far, to completing his purpose on earth, with respect to health and longevity, as the ape, the baboon, or the monkey.

We behold the seasons so beautifully balanced; we observe how the fowls of the air, the fishes of the sea, and the beasts of the field fit so perfectly into the scheme of Nature; we see that even the spider and the snake, except for the interference of man, are perfectly related to their environment. But man seems to be an outcast and a renegade.

Created to have dominion over all visible things, man is, instead, completely controlled and dominated by habits and environment. From the master of the visible realm, he has become the slave of the fear, stupidity, superstition, lustfulness, and wickedness of all the earth. He knows nothing of that Faith which would enable him, so to speak, to move the mountains from his path. He permits pleasure, fear, and superstition to supply the motive for his every action. His passage through the world is apparently divorced from all law and order, and governed solely by accident and chance. Instead of his being a part Of Nature, as are the lower animals, he is a part FROM Nature. His maxim seems to be-

## Any Way but the Natural Way!

From beginning to end, man lives and leads an unnatural life. He is continually doing things that war against Nature, thus placing both in an unnatural position, as to each other. This deranges a healthy body, disturbs its natural function, and destroys that quiet equipoise so necessary for a long, healthy, happy life. His mind, instead of being clean, calm, and serene, is clouded and perverted by traditional lustfulness, fear, and superstition. His body, which he should respect, reverence, and well-treat, is misused and abused beyond description.

The art of eating, which was designed merely to supply the body with needed nutrition, man has degraded into the most sensual pleasure. The peaceful slumber, so necessary to enable the body to recuperate after a hard day's toil, he too often thrusts aside to make way for what he deems a good time. Lastly, the procreative function that marvelous power bestowed by the Creator on man, in order that he may perpetuate himself and fulfill the injunction — Be fruitful, and multiply, and replenish the earth *(Genesis 1:28),* he has desecrated, debased, and profaned in the most despicable manner. Of this crime against the Creator and Nature one writer observes:

"Man is the highest form of all living creatures on earth, but by his sex nature he falls below the brutes. The brute does not defile its body, but man squanders his very life. Sensuality destroys body and mind, and shortens life.

"The pollution of sex comes between man and his God. The sensual do not love God, for they cannot serve God. The word of God has no attraction for such. God cannot be approached while the temple, in which the Kingdom of Heaven should be, is being polluted.

"There is no question on which people express and exhibit so much ignorance and which causes so much misery, sickness, and early death, as the ignorant abuse of sex matters.

"The physical decline is in proportion to the sexual waste. We cannot evade this fundamental truth. Every individual bears the marks of the truthfulness of this assertion. And the pollution of the temple or body is in ratio to the sexual degeneracy or other sinful practices."

Are infirmity and disease natural to man? In order that the weak may become strong, and the sick may become well, is it necessary to get power from without? Many men so think, for from them we hear this sort of reasoning: My body is weak from its birth, congenitally of a feeble nature, and for this reason there is no possibility of its becoming a healthy physique. The proof of this is found in the fact, that no matter how nutritious the food I eat, what various exercises I take, nor where I go for health, not the least improvement appears.

It is also usual to hear the same sort of complaint from those who are ordinarily distressed with sickness. They say, No matter what prominent physician I consult, nor what expensive medicine or treatment I take, there is no end to my disease; frequently when one disease has begun to be cured, I am attacked by another, and I am unable to forget the pains and illness for a single day. Why is this? Really, we men seem to be captives of disease, and since I appear to have no way of escape, I have now become resigned.

Indeed, as they have concluded that disease and infirmity dog them wherever they go, and that there is an evil affinity that can never be shaken off, their lot is a most pitiable one. If it be so that what they say is the truth without mistake, that when one has once become ill, escape is by no means possible, and the weak one can never again become robust, verily, is not man the most contemptible creature in the world?

While this state is the real condition of most men, it is not the actual condition of all men — nor is it the natural condition of any man. After the Creator had made the world and all living things, except man, He saw that it was good. He then wrought His grandest handiwork — Created man in his own (Spiritual) image *(Genesis 1:27),* made him king of the visible realm, and gave him dominion over the fish of the sea, and over the fowl of the air, and over every living thing that moveth upon the earth *(Genesis 1:28).*

From the hand of his Creator came man, perfect in organization and beautiful in form. His decline from that ideal state resulted directly from his own disobedient acts — destructive habits. The fact that he has for countless centuries withstood ever-increasing wear and tear of bodily disorders, produced by his own harmful habits, is conclusive proof of the wonderful power of endurance with which he was first endowed.

# Chapter No. 33
# Doctrine of Vicarious Atonement

The degraded condition of man, the highest work of creation, indicates that he has lost his way, and needs someone, some thing, some power, some guidance, to redeem him from the darkness in which he is wandering.

Therefore, came the Son of man to save that which was lost *(Matthew 18:11)*. He shed his blood for many *(Mark 14:24)*, just as other martyrs had before, and have since, that men might know the truth that makes them free from the creeds and dogmas of a lost world *(Luke 19:10; John 3:17)*. He came as a light of the world, that those who would believe in his teaching should not walk in darkness, but should enjoy the light of life *(John 8:12)*.

He brought light to the lost part of creation, that it might find the truth that would make it free. Man, lost in false belief, was to be shown the light, and be released from darkness. But the multitude thought Christ spoke of the material man, and answered that they were never in bondage to any one *(John 8:32-33)*. They were then in absolute bondage to their false belief, and still are; and so is the entire Christian world; and it will so remain, as long as it believes in the absurd atonement theory.

The Christian religion is based on the doctrine of Vicarious Atonement. This means that someone else can rescue or redeem us from sin by taking our sins upon himself, by becoming responsible for our wrongs, by suffering in the place of, or for the sake of another who has committed a crime. The Christian world, living in this belief, regards Christ as the Great Redeemer, the Saviour of a lost world.

It is the weak that cry for help. It is the man who depends on help that fails. We may offer a score of excuses for our failure, yet the fact remains that we failed; and we failed because we were not equal to the work confronting us. The man, who meets his task with a strong heart and a willing hand, is the man who succeeds; and we do not find such a man looking for help, praying for someone else to do what the Creator made him capable of doing, then placed his work before him.

To hold that God made man, then, placed him in an environment that would destroy him, or which he lacked strength to subdue, is to hold that God is an incompetent being. Neither do we believe that God, or the Infinite Intelligence that rules the Universe, made the earth, covered it with millions of living forms, and allowed the situation to get so far beyond his control, that he was constrained to send a Messenger in the Flesh to redeem, save, and bring back what he had made and lost.

The so-called atonement seems to be based chiefly on the following statement:

That it might be fulfilled which was spoken by Esaias the prophet, saying Himself took our infirmities, and bare our sickness *(Matthew 8:17)*.

This refers in particular to the 53rd Chapter of Isaiah, in which it is held that the subsequent suffering of Christ for man was foretold. From that chapter we select the following verses:

Surely he hath borne our griefs, and carried our sorrows *(vs. 4)*. Yet it pleased the Lord to bruise him; he hath put him to grief; when thou shalt make his soul an offering for sin *(vs. 10)*.

This is the straw at which the drowning man is clutching. It may be better to grasp at a straw than at nothing at all; but the drowning man would come nearer being saved, if he disregarded the tempting straw and used the powers his God gave him in an effort to save himself.

But contemplate how much easier it is for someone else to save us, than for us to save ourselves. Paul, in his various Epistles, disclosed the fact that he believed in saving his own strength, and allowing someone else to save him. He was a strong believer in, and a staunch supporter of, the doctrine of vicarious atonement. He wrote:

But God commendeth his love toward us, in that, while we were yet sinners, Christ died for us *(Romans 5:8)*.

Peter also "clutched at the straw," and believed that — Christ hath suffered for us in the flesh *(1 Peter 4:1)*; yet he flatly denied that he knew "the man" whom a short time before he had declared was — The Christ, the Son of the living God *(Matthew 16:16)*, and whom it is said that he saw — Transfigured before them and his face did shine as the sun, and his raiment was white as the light *(Matthew 17:2)*.

This is the same Peter who said: Lord, I am ready to go with thee, both into prison, and to death *(Luke 22:33)*. And again: Lord. Why cannot I follow thee now? I will lay down my life for thy sake *(John 13:37)*.

And when this same Peter was accused of being acquainted with Christ — Then began he to curse and to swear, saying, I know not the man *(Matthew 26:74)*.

When the time came to test the force of Peter's statements, they were found to be empty sounds — hollow as a rotten log. Contemplating this man earnestly declaring to his Christ — To whom shall we go? Thou hast the words of eternal life *(John 6:68)*. And then, when accused of being acquainted with Christ, this same man, this great Peter, cursed, and swore, and said, "I know not the man."

Peter — a "rock." This is the rock upon which I will build my church *(Matthew 16:18)*. If Christ was the man we believe he was that statement was not made by him. For Peter was a man of weak, impulsive, vacillating disposition. He was also a liar and a coward, according to the biblical account of his conduct.

What a "rock" on which to found a monument of truth. Can the building be greater than its foundation? Can a rock that crumbles into despicable dust under the force of the first preliminary test, be a safe place on which to erect one's hopes of "eternal life?" And this is the "rock" on which rests the institution that hopes to be saved through the blood of a rejected and murdered martyr. Unless saved in that way, it is certain that it will never be saved.

Leaving Peter and going to Paul, we first observe that his former name was Saul, meaning destroyer *(Acts 13:9)*, and this appellation appears to have been a very appropriate one, based on his own admission. For he was originally an avowed and implacable foe of the "disciples of the Lord," and says himself that he persecuted this way unto the death, binding and delivering into prisons both men and women *(Acts 22:4)*, for the very serious crime of believing in the teachings of the One whom he later regarded as having "died for him."

Breathing out ominous threatening and slaughter against the disciples of the Lord, Saul, who seems to have been some sort of an officer of the law, consenting unto Stephen's death, making havock of the church, entering into every house, and haling men and women, committed them to prison *(Acts 8:1-3)*, went unto the high priest, and desired of him letters to Damascus to the synagogues, authorizing him to bring bound unto Jerusalem, such men and women as he found that were believers in the teachings of Christ *(Acts 9:1-2)*.

But even the hardened criminal at last reaches the point, where he can no longer bear the "pricks" of his own guilty conscience, and he experiences a change of heart, and reforms. Saul underwent this change on the highway to Damascus. As he journeys along the hot, dusty road with his servants, he is alone with his terrible thoughts. He has time to reflect on the heinous crimes that he has committed, and of the horrors of his present errand. Being only human after all, he began to sicken at the contemplation of the suffering and misery that he was causing, and believed that this was a favorable opportunity for him to make a change and become a better man. Who wouldn't?

But how was he to escape from his present predicament? He had boldly stalked into the frowning presence of the high priest, loudly stated his bloody intentions, and requested a commission authorizing him to carry out his murderous work. Perchance, before such letters were granted, he had been required to take a solemn oath, with a drastic penalty to be imposed for his failure to perform his task.

However, he seems to have been equal to the occasion. As he drew near Damascus, suddenly there shined around about him a light from heaven, so he says; and that he fell to the earth, and heard a voice saying unto him, Saul, Saul, why persecutes thou me? And he said, who arc thou, Lord? And the Lord said, I am Jesus whom thou persecutes *(Acts 9:44)*. And so the story goes. If you have not read it, then read it.

Saul knew that there was at Damascus a certain disciple named Ananias. No doubt Ananias was the principal person that Saul had hoped to bring bound unto Jerusalem, for delivery into prison. But since his change of heart, he is now going to use his intended victim for a far different purpose. For he enters into a plot with Ananias, for the purpose of carrying out his designs of proselyting; and he concocted one of the best fish yarns that we have ever read, in order to perform his plan.

Most any of us can fabricate a fairly good story as to our motive for taking a certain course, when we are ready to make such a complete about-face. And we can improve on that story when we think of the taunting jeers and sneers that we know will be hurled at us for yielding to such a great change of heart. We would be constrained to give the best reasons we could think of; and Saul seems to have been an artist, when it came to manufacturing fish-stories.

What did Paul know about Christ and his doctrine? He was quite a young man when the Master was engaged in his work *(Acts 7:58)*. People of tender years are not, as a rule, seriously affected by religion. They are sportive, vivacious, and adventurous. Their attention is turned to the light, shallow, and exciting sides of life. It is the more mature men who, feeling the weight of passing years, turn to investigate the probable "destination of the soul after death." Paul was engaged in the work of persecution and murder, not because of the religious aspect of the situation, but because of the excitement it afforded.

Paul never saw Christ. He gathered his information from the disciples, most of whom were illiterate fishermen. The veracity of fishermen is very low today, and we have no reason to assume that it was higher then. The biblical account shows that they had all the weaknesses of other men. Their hearts were set on earthly things; they were envious and jealous, and quarreled with one another. Each wanted to be greatest in the temporal kingdom, which they thought Christ was about to establish.

The minds of the disciples were so steeped in things material, that they seldom understood the Master's sayings *(John 10:6)*. Growing impatient with their gross, material conceptions of his teachings, Christ sharply demanded of them, Are ye also yet without understanding *(Matthew 15:16)?*

From this source came Paul's information of the doctrine of Christ. On this hearsay evidence, from illiterate fishermen, who understood not the teaching of their Master, and showed by their questions and conduct that they did not understand it, Paul, assuming to know more about Christ than anyone else, proceeds to construct his theory of vicarious atonement — and our songbooks and our sermons arc filled with the teaching and the thought —

But God commended, his love toward us, in that, while we were yet sinners. Christ died for us *(Romans 1:8)*.

The reason that Paul took the leading part in the play, is because he was the only one that had the education necessary to performs the task. He was an educated Jew of a well-to-do family, and had been instructed in the principal learning of his time. So it was his ability to perform the task, and not his knowledge of Christ and his doctrine that made him the leading light in the work.

The most absurd theory of the doctrine of Vicarious Atonement that we have found is related by W. E. Van Amburgh, and we shall give it here:

"Christ was God's first son; and after he was created, he was associated with God in all the further works of creation. He was neither divine nor immortal until he had proved his worthiness to receive such honors. Now he is divine. A correct understanding of the true relationship between the Father and the Son, and of what God has done for Christ, clarifies much of what before was impossible to understand. We now see something of the value of the prize set before Christ; his great victory in overcoming the temptations of world number two. The heavenly host declared that he was worthy. Who would not count it a privilege to win such a prize, if the opportunity were offered?

"Truth is often stranger than fiction. What shall we say when we learn that God has actually made a similar offer to others, that if they desire to run the same race, they may win a similar crown?

"Let us stop here a minute to get a clearer view of the manner in which God carried out his plan to bring all this about. God gave the Children of Israel a law, that if one did an injury to another, ravishment would be demanded in equal kind: An eye for an eye; a tooth for a tooth; hand for hand;

foot for foot; life for life *(Exodus 21:23-25)*. Adam disobeyed, and lost his life. If Adam is ever to receive any blessing in the future, he will have to be awakened from death and brought back to life. How can this be, and at the same time the demands of justice, calling for a 'life for life,' remain satisfied?

"Let us make a little parable. Suppose a farmer owned a sheep that had been bad, and was condemned to die. Suppose the owner of the sheep also had a fine shepherd dog and, after explaining that the disobedient sheep must die unless some other sheep die in its place, would make this proposition to him: 'Trust, if you will agree to let me transform you from a dog into a sheep, and then consent to die in the place of that sheep, I will then transform you into a man like myself.'

"Here would be a proposition for Trust to consider. If he consents, the master changes him into a sheep. This is a complete change of nature. He is not part dog and part sheep, but all sheep. Then, instead of letting the first sheep be put to death, the master puts the second one to death in its place. The life of one sheep has been given for the life of the other sheep. That releases the first sheep, and permits it to live. The law is complied with.

"But what about sheep number two, the one which had been a dog? His master had promised that he should be brought to life as a man. The master keeps his promise. Sheep number two died as a sheep, but is resurrected as a man. What a change! Was not the prize of securing human life worth the suffering as a sheep? How much better to be a man than a shepherd dog. No injustice is done any one. Sheep number one is set free; the dog humbled himself to become a sheep, then died as a sheep, and was rewarded for his sacrifice by being exalted to be a man. He would never want to be a dog or a sheep again. The law holds the life of a sheep as punishment for the transgression; so the law is satisfied.

"Jesus occupied a very high position in heaven, but humbled himself and took the form of a man, to die as a man for Adam; and God rewarded him by giving him a much higher position and nature than he had held before."

The above proposition is based on *Philippians 2:6-10,* as interpreted by Diglot, according to Van Amburgh. Another example of the turning and twisting of words, in order to manufacture support for our theories and philosophies.

Van Amburgh continues:

"Adam was under sentence of death. It would take a human life to ransom him. Jesus agreed to be changed into a man, and become a perfect man, such as Adam was before he sinned. Jesus died in the place of Adam, thus giving his life as a perfect man as a ransom for Adam. Adam now can be freed when the time comes, and be resurrected to life again. Jesus will never be a man again; for God has given him a much better life. The dog could not use a dog body and live as a man; neither can Jesus use a human body and live as a divine being. 'Flesh and blood cannot inherit the kingdom of God' *(1 Corinthians 15:50).* Justice is satisfied. It has the life of a perfect man to take the place of the perfect man who sinned."

But did Jesus die in the place of Adam? Adam died and his body returned "unto the ground," just as related in *Genesis 3:19.* His body has been dust now for to these many ages. We should like to have Van Amburgh explain how Adam is to be "resurrected to life again." In another place we have stated why "flesh and blood cannot inherit the kingdom of God."

Van Amburgh further says:

"Let us go back a moment to our parable of the dog and the sheep. The dog entered into a contract that he was first to be changed from a dog to a sheep. Then he was to die as a sheep. Death might come by disease and pain, or drowning, or even by hanging. The contract called for death, the manner not stated. He was then to be resurrected as a man. Fit knew that he could not retain his dog body and become a sheep. Nor could he retain his sheep body and become a man. He must pass through two complete changes of nature. It would therefore make no difference in the end by what means he died as a sheep; for die he must."

Observe how material this author is. His every thought is steeped in materialism. He speaks of position, and high position, and the promotion of Jesus because he proved to be a trustworthy and faithful employee. He speaks of agreements and contracts, which must be fulfilled and satisfied. He refers to a law, which God gave the Children of Israel, and then he takes Christ, God's first son, changes him from a "very high position in heaven," to the form of man on earth, puts him to death, resurrects him and transforms him into something else than a human body, because "flesh and blood cannot inherit the kingdom of God."

These changes and transformations take place in defiance of all law, for law is a rule of action that occurs always and ever the same, without variation, change, or exception. So that the "contract that called for death," Van Amburgh has fulfilled by the most flagrant violation of law that could be imagined. He calls this 'Truth (which) is often stranger than fiction." This is the brand of truth and religion that is proposed to save "souls."

"A guilty man needs no accuser." Man knows in his heart that he is not obeying the law. If you should ask him in what way he is disobeying the law, perchance he could not tell you. And yet he knows that he is violating the law in some way. How does he know it? By his guilty conscience; by the conditions of misery and suffering with which he is surrounded. He realizes in some apparently unexplainable manner that this is not as it should be, but he does not know how to remedy the situation. He would not be looking for a savior if he did not think that he needed a savior.

It is through his soul-spirit-life that man knows he is violating the law. But instead of his heeding the warning of the soul, and learning the law and obeying it, he remains ignorant of the law, daily violates it, and continues in a forced belief of the doctrine of Vicarious Atonement,

As to his aspect of religion William R. Reece says:

"The central idea of the Christian religion, as almost universally accepted at present, is the 'Vicarious Atonement.' This, as is known to all in Christian lands, is the idea that Christ, the second person in the trinity, died on the cross to save us from the penalty of sin, and that if we believe on Him and believe that He did thus die for us, we shall certainly be saved from the wrath to come.

"It is also taught, that man can do nothing of himself to save himself, and that the pure spinelessness of the Son of God is imputed (or made over) to all sincere believers, so that they are thenceforth regarded by God the Father as without sin — the spinelessness of the Christ being miraculously transferred to them.

"Without going into a lengthy theological argument, let me say that this 'scheme of salvation' implies a deity external to man (or two of them, sometimes even three in the thought of many). It implies that man is entirely powerless to help himself, and it also implies that a third thing must come between man and sin, and save him from the penalty of violated laws, by taking the brunt of violated law on itself. This is the "Vicarious Atonement," the suffering of another, the suffering of the Son of God, in the stead of the sinner." (*Health For All*).

Says Doctor H. M. Shelton:

"For hundreds of years, humanity has believed and preached a false system of ethics. They have held that a fault may be atoned for by suffering that has no direct connection with, and does not rise out of, the fault. Every one may atone for his faults by penance, or by the purchase of indulgences, or someone else may suffer for him. It is equivalent to to the belief that one can put his hand in the fire and another be burned for him.

"The old idea of Christ's sacrifice was that I sin and Christ suffers for me. The old doctrine of hell was that I sin now and suffer in the hereafter. There was no necessary connection between my present sinning and my future suffering. The sin does not produce the suffering, and I would escape suffering for my sin except for the agency of a third thing that inflicts the punishment upon me. I was to be punished FOR my sins, not BY them" (*How To Live For Health and Strength,* May, 1926).

Pastor Russell writes a volume of 490 words, entitled *The Atonement Between God and Man,* in which he juggles words and phrases in every conceivable manner to show that there is — One mediator between God and men, the man Christ Jesus; who gave himself a ransom for all, to be testified in due time *(1 Timothy 2:5-6).*

And he quotes these words: "The Son of Man came to give his life a ransom for many" *(Mark 10:45).*
And then he observes:

"There is no room for quibbling or disputing the meaning of these texts. Only by handling the Word of God deceitfully can any be blinded to the force and real meaning of this, the Lord's testimony to the work which has been accomplished by our great Mediator. And the more this thought of a ransom — a 'corresponding price' — is considered, the more force does it seem to contain, and the more light does it shed upon the entire work of the Atonement.

"The thought, and the only thought, contained in it is, that as Adam, through disobedience, forfeited his being, his soul, all his rights to life and to earth, so Christ Jesus our Lord, by his death, as a corresponding price, paid a full and exact offset for Father Adam's soul or being, and in consequence for all his posterity — every human soul — shares in his fall and in his loss" — *Romans 1:12.*

Of these who do not believe in the "ransom," as he does, Pastor Russell says:

"The many foes of the doctrine of the ransom, of whom the chief is Satan, sometimes with great cunning attempt to divert the attention away from the price given for man's release from the curse of death, by pointing out those texts of Scripture in which the words 'redeem' and 'redemption' are applied merely as relating to the full deliverance of mankind from death.

"By calling attention to the deliverance, and 'handling the Word of God deceitfully,' they attempt to obscure the fact that the future deliverance, and all the blessings that now or in the futures will conic to mankind by divine grace, are of the Son, and through or by means of the ransom-sacrifice of himself, which he gave. in our behalf, and which was 'finished' at Calvary. — (*John 19:30*).

"The translators of our Common Version English Bible unwittingly aided these opponents of the ransom, by using the word 'redeem' to translate Greek words which have considerably different meanings" (*The Atonement, etc.*, page 429).

The Great Teacher was a remarkable man. His earnest, thoughtful, profound, spiritual preachments were too deep for his material audiences. The truths he uttered are not found in institutions. "Lay not up for yourselves treasures upon earth" are sentiments not tolerated by schools of theology.

Jesus was a Jew; but from the law of his people he got no inspiration. Desire for place and power was not his. In his great simplicity he rose above banker, preacher, professor, doctor, and lawyer. He was bound by no creed; he founded no sect. Dividing truth was, to him, impossible; for a half truth is as dangerous as an error.

Eloquent in speech and in silence; shunning the rich and self-seekers, he sought the lowly, needy, and sickly — for they that be whole need not a physician. To these his poise, presence, and kindness was a tremendous inspiration. For forty miles around, the maimed, sick, and blind heard of this kind, unselfish man, of whom no harm was spoken; and they flocked to him in hope and confidence, as they would to any man of similar character and reputation. And his unlimited faith in the infinite benevolence of the Father of all creation enabled him to make a profound impression upon them.

He was the avowed enemy of the wealthy and powerful, the priests, the scribes, and the "money changers" (bankers). This drew to his banner the outcast, the lepers, and the poor.

Arrayed against him was the "powers that be," and so from the beginning, he knew his fate. But he had no family, no property, no worldly ambitions, so he did not care for life. He learned of the fate of his cousin, John, but he continued to ridicule the rulers with withering scorn.

As long as he preached love and lowliness, he was safe. The rulers and leaders objected not to his doctrine of loving your enemies, and turning "the other check" to the smiter. But when he began openly to denounce the priests and scribes as "hypocrites," and "thieves," and "vipers," it was high time for them to act. So they invoked their barbaric law.

In the mob that assembled and demanded his blood, he had not a friend who dared speak out. His disciples, liars and cowards all but John, had denied him and fled. He was taunted, scorned, and insulted. Truth and Light had played and lost. Iniquity and hypocrisy has added another scalp to its bloody belt. The lowly Nazarene hung limp upon the cross, and the first stone of the Christian church was laid. Bickering began at once. The Romans blamed the Jews for the bloody act, and the Jews blamed the Romans. The seed had been sown for the destruction of nations.

His biographers made him ridiculous, and marred the beauty of his career by distorting the facts with their own false conceptions and opinions. They wrote from the current legends of the illiterate peasants, who were educated to believe in magic and mystery, in sorcery and necromancy, in ghosts and goblins, in demons and devils.

These simple folks believed that God, who made the world, also made a competitor in the shape of Satan, who outguessed, outgeneraled, and outwitted the Maker. Competition between Satan and God was keen. Sateen was an adroit schemer, and God lacked executive ability to handle the situation. He acknowledged defeat by delegating the work to his "son," who also acknowledged defeat on the cross when he said, "Father forgive them, for they know not what they do." As the whole affair had been turned over to him, according to the teaching of the church, why did he not do the forgiving?

If Christ came in the office of a "redeemer of men," why did Christ give so little attention to a thing so important? If this was his chief office, why was the thought not his chief topic?

Those who write of him, with the exception of Matthew, Mark, Luke, and John, make the redemption of man, through the blood and suffering of Christ, the leading topic of their theme. And even the four mentioned, because of their material belief, turned and twisted words and phrases in order to bring out as much as possible this thought.

That Christ did not make the doctrine of vicarious atonement the principal topic of his teaching, should give no little concern to the advocates of the doctrine. It should give them a feeling of no little discomfort; for, have they not hung their hopes of eternal life on a very frail limb?

But men are men; and are as blind now as at any time in the history of humanity. They think for themselves now, no more than they did in the days of Christ. Thinking is the hardest task under the sun. Rather than think, men believe in the teachings of others, whether it be right or wrong. As to that part of the teaching, they give no thought. They are too weak to think. They lean on the thought of others. They grasp at anything for help, regardless how frail that thing may be, rather than exert a little effort in self-help.

He that heareth my word, and believeth on him that sent me, hath (now) everlasting life, and is passed (now) from death unto life. Can any stretch of the wildest imagination construe these statements into meaning that Christ came and died to save sinful men, or that by his blood they are "washed whiter than snow?"

We have observed how the Bible was compiled for the purpose of supporting certain phases of religious teaching. And history relates how the institution of religion took the teaching of Christ, and with it plunged the world into the most terrible darkness that man has record of. The astonishing part of the proposition is the general belief of this day in this land, that men are free from these blasting influences.

The murderous element that slew Christ saw that their designs were going to be defeated, that his end would not stop the spread of the truths he taught. So it became necessary to devise other measures for the preservation of their dominion over the people. Taking the truths proclaimed by Christ to a lost world, they canonized them, and made of them a foundation on which to erect their degrading institution. Yes, the chief priest, the elders, and the scribes took the words "of spirit and of life" uttered by the lowly Carpenter of Nazareth, and wove them into a cable of steel, and used them to bind the burden of a false religion on the bending back of oppressed humanity — and this they did in the very name of the humble One they crucified.

The priesthood took the message of Spirit and of Truth, and from it taught a new perversion in the blood of thousands, to the darkness of nations, which darkness reached its pinnacle during the sixteenth century in the "awful Massacre of St. Bartholomew, in August, 1572." Of this John Abbott observes:

"As we see the priests of Paris and of France, during the awful tragedy of the (French) Revolution, massacred in the prisons, shot in the streets, hung upon the lamp-posts, and driven in starvation and woe from the kingdom, we cannot but remember the day of St. Bartholomew. The 24th of August, 1572, and the 2nd of September, 1792, though far apart in the records of time, are consecutive days in the government of God."

We are peculiarly impressed with some observations of Joseph McCabe regarding the Bible. We shall quote him:

"Two thousand five hundred years after the great King Nebuchadnezzar lay on his gold and ivory couch, and cursed these (Hebrew) savages of the Syrian hills, the fragments of his mighty empire and its culture would be patiently dug out of the dust, while the sacred book of the Jews would be kissed reverently all over the world, in the law-courts of prouder cities than Persian or Babylonian ever saw."

"The Old Testament, together with the New Testament, rules us — is read with honor in the very modern schools of America, is handled reverently in courts, closes theaters on a Sunday in England, and so on — solely because hundreds of millions of people, before whom politicians tremble and editors dissemble, believe that it is 'the Word of God'" (*The Forgery of the Old Testament,* (page 8).

Why do "hundreds of millions of people" believe that the Bible is "the Word of God?" Let us tell you — According to press reports of July 10, 1927, The Baptists' Bible Union of North America, in control of the Des Moines (Iowa) University, has decreed that the faculty members must subscribe to "the eighteen articles of faith." Among the principal tenets of the "eighteen articles of faith" are:

1 - Belief in the Bible as the infallible word of God;
2 - That it was written by man supernaturally inspired;
3 - Belief in Genesis account of creation;
4 - Belief in the virgin birth of Christ;
5 - Belief in the resurrection of Christ;
6 - Belief that the whale swallowed Jonah.

No man is able to imagine the stupidity and bigotry that must govern an institution which forces teachers of this the 20th century A. D. to acknowledge as the infallible Word of God, an absurd Jewish mythology of antiquity, originating with people who believe in all sorts of sorcery and mystery. It is beyond the imagination of any one, who has the capacity to comprehend the spiritual meaning underlying the teaching of Christ, to conceive of the degree of dogmatism and fanaticism which must rule these who perform such preposterous acts as here indicated.

This is a typical illustration of the way that religion has always endeavored to obstruct human enlightenment. The progress of mankind faces no graver danger than that of such obstinate conduct. Humanity cannot advance in knowledge as long as a corps of enslaved teachers must force down the public throat, a belief in things so erroneous as to be inconsistent with every lesson that we learn from every plant and every tree.

If we labor for a livelihood, we must obey the mandates of our employers. If our office is that of teaching, those we tutor come to us to learn, and will of course believe the things we teach. If we with apparent sincerity teach them that "the whale swallowed Jonah," it becomes a part of their belief, and is passed on from father to son. And thus the belief of "hundreds of millions of people" is the belief of a sordid institution, which uses this means to keep the shackles of bondage on the limbs of man, for the sole benefit of that institution.

It is true that conditions have somewhat improved since the burning of Bruno. In the United States and some few other countries, no longer can men be legally burned, crucified, and imprisoned for disputing the Bible, edited and canonized by a deceitful, lying priesthood for an ignoble purpose. But we perceive that "the powers that be" are determined that the shackles of bondage shall be kept on the limbs of man, regardless of the darkness into which such course leads.

So we observe why men still believe in the teaching of Christ, as debased, biased, warped, and twisted by his murderous foes, and as expounded for a price from the pulpit by those who seek this course as an easy means of a livelihood. And a fawning, subservient public press, so slavish in its desires to please "the powers that be" and of which press Senator Robert L. Owen, on the floor of the United States Senate in April, 1924, declared — CAN BE

USED TO SUPPRESS, DISTORT, AND MISLEAD, that same press will discredit and brand as dangerous radicals and rascals, any man or set of men who express the least disbelief in the teaching of Christ, as debased, warped, and twisted by his slayers.

The most preposterous part of the whole proposition is, that the Christ they murdered, "redeemed" their selfish, sorid, sinful souls by and through the very life which they took, the very blood which they shed.

Why, the gross absurdity of the doctrine of vicarious atonement, the redemption of man through the blood of a murdered Christ, woven through and through the works and the writings of the cunning advocates of this belief, stands without equal in the entire annals of human thought. All we have of the teaching of Christ is based on hearsay evidence from witnesses who could not understand the meaning of the Master's word, and who deserted and denied the Master when his enemies took him. If these witnesses did not themselves believe, yet being eye-witnesses we are told, how can we at this late day believe, when we must base our belief on the hearsay evidence of those who believed not?

Hearsay evidence is a kind of evidence that is not admitted in any court of law. It does not drive its value solely from the credit to be attached to the witness himself, but rests also in part on the veracity and competency of some other person, from whom the witness received his information. It is inadmissible because not given under the sanction of an oath, and not subject to cross-examination.

Men living on the material plane, thinking on the material plane, knowing nothing of the spiritual, having visions of material grandeur, are little fitted to relate or write an account of the words of Spirit and of Life, uttered by the

Master they heard, but not understood by them. For they will warp and twist words in every possible manner, so as to fabricate support for their material beliefs. And their readers, if also materialists, will further warp and twist the written word, in order to gain support for their material opinions.

We do read that the Son of man is come to save that which was lost *(Matthew 18:11)*. Admitting that Christ made that statement, or one of similar import, shall we cast aside all the rest of his teaching and hang our hopes of eternal life on this lone limb?

Christ had in mind always the spiritual part of man, which is Life. But the disciples had in mind the material man only. They could think only of material things; they could not understand him. Said he, Are ye also yet without understanding? *(Matthew 15:16)*.

He came to save that which was lost. The spiritual man was lost, because he was not recognized. Man, made of dust, thought he was Life. Laboring under this delusion, he fell to the worship of reptiles, calves, idols, and unknown gods. He was unable to connect his existence with his Creator. He had gone astray he was, indeed, lost.

All other living creatures, in their own peculiar way, understand the relation between them and the Father. They to this day trust the Father to supply all their needs. Take no thought of what ye shall eat or drink, nor of raiment. Even the flowers of the field toil not, neither do they spin; and yet their needs are fully supplied by the One by which they live and trust. But of all living things, man, of little faith, was and is the only sheep that has gone astray.

Man is lost. He has missed the strait gate and the narrow way which leadeth unto life, and has entered the wide gate and the broad way, that leadeth to destruction *(Matthew*

*7:13-14).* He thinks he is Life, and he has given himself up to the lust of the flesh. He has fallen to the lowest depths of all created things. Relatively speaking, the beasts of the field, in their conduct and observance of the law, are saints compared to man.

Man is lost. He has vastly degenerated from the high plane of mental, moral, and physical perfection on which the Father placed him. Christ tried to help him back, and his word was not believed. Many others have tried to lift man up out of the mire; but they have been murdered, and their works and writings debased and destroyed.

The teaching of the doctrine of 'vicarious atonement' has had and is having a vast influence in hastening the degenerative process that long ago seized humanity. No greater calamity could befall the race, than the thought that man, lost by his own conduct, is saved from the penalty of his wrongs through the "blood of the Redeemer."

How easy for weak men to believe such nonsense, and how difficult for them to forsake their vices, which have mastered them, and perform for themselves the service of self-help. So the ranks of the Vicarious Atonement advocates are well filled, and the leaders wax fat on the substance of a credulous people.

The sole aim and end of all religion, regardless of its denomination, is to gain "eternal life." But how gain it? By so living as to be worthy of it? By ceasing to do evil and learning to do well? By ceasing to be one of those riotous eaters of festering flesh *(Proverbs 23:20),* and eating fruit instead? By giving up tea, coffee, soda-fountain-slops, alcoholic beverages, etc., and drinking only water and fresh fruit juices? By ceasing to be fornicators and adulterers *(1 Corinthians 6:9),* and using the genital organs for the sole, single, and sacred purpose of perpetuating the race *(Genesis 1:28)?* By thinking constructive thoughts and by loving our fellow man, instead of having hearts filled with hatred, jealousy, and evil continually *(Genesis 6:5)?*

No; your guess is wrong, and your confidence misplaced. Man is willing to be "saved," if the "saving" can be done by leaving him undisturbed in his disobedience and wickedness. But if he must obey the law in order to be "saved," then he does not want to be saved. This is proved by every phase of religion, and by all past experience, and by the daily conduct of the most sanctified Christian leaders and followers. They want to be "saved," if someone else can do the "saving" of them for them, and provided the "saving" does not interfere with their daily habits of living.

# Chapter No. 34
# Return To Obedience

The curse upon mankind, as it is generally understood and preached, is a future curse of eternal torment — not a present curse. But according to the Scriptures it is a present curse, viz., death, which will be lifted in the future (Pastor Russell in *The Atonement,* etc., page 405).

The body of man, in the beginning, if not now, was perfectly constructed in each and every detail for the duty it was designed to perform. It was endowed with capacity to receive sufficient intelligence from the Infinite Source, to enable it to live in health and happiness in the environment in which it was placed; and it was further endowed with the potentiality of eternal existence, as we have observed. Its decline and decay from that perfect state, and its disintegration and death, were brought about, not by any inherent defects in its construction and operation, as physicians would have us believe, but by the maltreatment of it by its owner.

To live long means to obey the law in living. But even under ideal conditions, the length of time that the body will endure depends quite largely upon the degree of mental and physical perfection inherited from the earthly parents. The children of mentally and physically defective and weakened parents must to a certainty be afflicted with the disabilities of the parents.

Man is not capable of bestowing on his offspring that which he does not have. Man, now so degraded and imperfect mentally, morally, and physically, must to a more or less extent pass these defects on to his children. Yet this does not mean that the existence even of a degenerated body cannot be lengthened by proper living — by obedience. Just as Cornaro, by right living, increased the length of his days by 62 years, when his body at 40 was at the brink of the grave; so every man, by following the same course, can greatly increase his life-span. And if this procedure be continued from generation to generation, we should soon have the father dying at 150, the son at 200, the grandson at 300, the great grandson at 400, and so on.

We must not be too optimistic and hope, by right living, to increase the life-span too greatly in one or two generations. Nor should we fall into discouragement and give up because progress seems slow. That the life-span can thus be increased, no one will dispute. And if it can be increased 62 years in one generation, as in the case of Cornaro, why not increased in the next, and the next, and so on, until eventually the span of human life would be back to 900 years. And why stop there? Why not continue building and improving, and finally reach, say the 1,000 or 2,000-year mark.

Contemplate what could be accomplished by such men as Christ, Bruno, Socrates, Galileo, Plato, Aristotle, Seneca, Plutarch, Newton, Washington, Lincoln, Trail, Edison, Burbank, were they to live five hundred or a thousand years. The present life-span of man is so ephemeral, that most men die before they really begin to live, and many pass on before that age is reached.

By observing how the ages of the men of the Bible decreased after the Flood, we see that the process was gradual with the race in general, as Noah died at 950, Shem at 600, Arphaxad at 465, and so on down. This is a splendid and reliable lesson which teaches that to the same extent the return will be a gradual process. Step by step, as it were, the length of human life, can, and some day will, be increased, up and up from the few short years that man now lives, to the grand old age of Methuselah.

Due to the eating and drinking of poisonous substances, to medicinal poisons that men take when ill, and to many other harmful habits that kill, the body is subjected to a continuous process of systematic poisoning from the moment of impregnation, and even long before, to the last heart-beat of existence. The body lasts as long as it can fight back and hold off the degenerating encroachment of this poisoning, and no longer. The variation exhibited in the length of human life, is dependent upon and governed by this condition. The less poison the body is forced to tolerate and endure, the longer will it last. That, in a nutshell, is the reason why one man dies at 50 while another lives 125 years.

Regardless of whether a man lives 25 years or 125, Life always leaves the Temple of Clay most reluctantly, and never until to remain longer becomes utterly impossible under the law which governs its operation. How long Life shall remain in the body, is determined by man's own conduct, and not by the number of times the sun passes over his head.

# Chapter No. 35
# Where is Hell?

What could we think of a God, who knows the end from the beginning, and who is said to be all love, that would make man to pass a life of misery here on earth, and then condemn his "soul" to everlasting punishment? Yet there is not a man in Christendom that does not believe in the doctrine of "everlasting torment," and there is not an orthodox preacher who does not preach it. The Catholic church dogmatically declares that the wicked will be tormented night and day forever and ever, without ceasing. "Throughout the countless ages of eternity their torture will know no end."

Where does this torture take place? In an unknown region called "hell." What does the word "hell" mean? It is an Anglo-Saxon word, which means to cover, to conceal, to hide, it is closely related to the word "hole."

While heaven was supposed to be located above, hell was said to be down-down where? down in the bowels of the earth. That was when the ancients believed that the earth was flat. Recent knowledge has shown that the world is round, that it turns on its axis, revolves around the sun, and floats in space. This has led the former believers in the existence of "hell" to grow somewhat skeptical, and they have been busy revising their opinions and theories.

The result is, that from the Revised Version the word "hell" disappears excepting in two places, where it is retained for a particular reason. In the R. V. it is replaced by the original words, which are three — (1) the Hebrew "sheol," with its Greek equivalent "hades." These two words are elastic and vague. They mean, generally, the place of the departed. Sometimes they are translated "pit," sometimes "grave."

(2) The second word of the R. V. replacing the A. V. word "hell" is the word "tartarus." This word occurs only twice-in the second Epistle of Peter, and the Epistle general

of Jude. It is the heathen word for hell, and is even less clear in meaning than either sheol or hades.

(3) The last change of this character made in the R. V. is the word "Gahanna." This occurs twelve times in the New Testament, eleven of these being in the first three Gospels.

Gahanna is really an abbreviation used for "the Vale of Hinnom," — Ge-Hinnom, a valley that lay to the south of Jerusalem. The story of this place is told in *2 Chronicles,* chapter 28 and 33.

At one time the Vale of Hinnom was a fair garden, where grew flowers, fruits, and vegetables. Later it became a place of idolatry. Children were thrown into a heated metal image and burned — they "passed through the fire" *(2 Chronicles 28:3; 33:6).* Men thought of Ge-Hinnom with a shudder.

When Josiah ascended the throne, he ordered the terrible idolatry stopped, and caused the vale to be held in horror. He "defiled it" by making it the great garbage-heap of Jerusalem. Dead bodies were consumed in the vale. Fires were kept burning night and day under the immense pile.

During the days of Christ, the Vale of Hinnom was still used in this way. This, then, is the meaning of the word "Gehenna." The word stood as a symbol of utter ruin, and that is the manner in which Christ used it.

So we observe that the words "sheol," "Hades," "tartarus," and "Gehenna," which lie back of the English word "hell," are simply symbolical expressions, and are not intended to convey any information concerning punishment and torment in "the life beyond the grave." And humanity is still searching for the "hell," in which Christendom believes.

> *Where's Hell? was asked a man one time,*
> *Who in a few words defined it.*
> *Why, that's what you build yourself,*
> *But Heaven's where you find it* — James Bryan

# Chapter No. 36
# Where is Heaven?

A vast change is springing up in men's minds regarding "the life beyond the grave." They are asking where is located "that undiscovered country, from whose bourne no traveler returns." As human knowledge broadens, men find confusion instead of solace in such statements as:

So when this corruptible shall have put on incorruption, and this mortal shall have put on immortality, then shall be brought to pass the saying that is written, Death is swallowed up in victory *(1 Corinthians 15:54)*.

It is not long since that preachers represented heaven and hell as fixed states and positive places. What authority had they for this? Where was their heaven? And where their hell? Heaven was up, hell was down. Just some more of the absurd beliefs of the ancients, still taught in the churches and preached from the pulpits.

To the ancient Greeks and Romans, the blue sky was a dome, above which lived the gods, and on the earth below, which they said was flat, lived men. At night they could see that the dome was pierced with many windows, and through these the gods above watched the works of men below. The Disciples of Christ grew up in this belief. It was a part of them just as fully and as completely as it was a part of the rest of mankind of that day in that land. So John has Christ saying — In my Father's house are many mansions; if it were not so, I would have told you. I go to prepare a place for you *(14:2)*.

And we are told that there was also a strife among the disciples, as to which of them should be accounted the greatest *(Mark 9:34; Luke 22:24)*. Of course the reason was, that the greatest of them would abide in the greatest of the mansions "in my Father's house." So it was well worth disputing and striving to gain honor of such greatness.

Luke closes his narrative of the work of Christ by observing: And it came to pass, while he blessed them, he was parted from them, and carried up into heaven *(24:11)*.

Mark states:

So then after the Lord had spoken unto them, he was received up into heaven, and sat on the right hand of God *(16:19)*.

We believe that God is within His kingdom, for where else would He be? When Luke says that Christ was "carried up into heaven," he seems to have forgotten his own statement of what Christ said as to the location of the "kingdom." He states: The kingdom of God cometh not with observation; for, behold, the kingdom of God is within you *(Luke 17:20-21)*.

Notwithstanding this clean cut statement, religionists continue to believe in heaven as a most beautiful place, lying beyond the grave, high up in the blue skies, and here the "soul" of man goes, after death, and enjoys endless happiness, provided he believed in his lifetime that "Christ was the son of God."

But if a man does not so believe; if, on the other hand, he has found the truth and been freed from the bondage of sects and creeds, and therefore, believes that the Law of the Universe never was and never will be violated; if he believes that every man has a material father and a material mother; if he believes that God is the one common Father of all men, and of all Creation; if he believes that a Christ is made by Christly living, and not by special creation — we say, if he believes these things, then religion classes him as a sinner, an infidel, a disbeliever in "the divine institution of

Christianity," and his "unbelieving soul" must go and repose in the black, bottomless pit, called "hell," and sizzle forever over the scorching heat of a ceaseless fire.

Increasing knowledge is threatening to destroy the belief in heaven that we have inherited from the ancients. The supposition that "heaven" is somewhere beyond the stars, a golden palace on the convex side of the firmament, has long been exploded by the discoveries of Astronomy alone. The telescope has shown that the "blue skies," above which was "the kingdom of heaven," is endless space, in which other worlds of marvelous size have been discovered.

Antares, one of the tiny specks of light floating in this limitless space, is said to be larger than the great path in space followed by the Earth in its sweep around the Sun. And the distance from the Earth to some of these giant worlds is so vast, that astronomers find it impossible to handle the immense numbers in trying to compute this distance, and, instead, use the light-year as a unit of measurement — which is the distance that light travels in a year, or about 63,000 times the distance of the Sun from the Earth. Some of these planets that have been discovered, are thousands of times larger than our Sun, and are removed from us by probably millions of light-years.

And in case we feel infinitesimally small in comparison of our Earth to such vastness, let us turn in the opposite direction and observe our giganticness by taking a peep into the tiny atom, which is the smallest particle of matter that we have so far been able to study.

The structure of the atom, as strange as it may appear, is on the same plan as the structure of the Universe. The positive nucleus, or the center of this tiny bit of matter, resembles the Sun, in that around it whirls at

incomprehensible speeds, the negative particles, the ions or
electrons. And these negative particles are, relatively
speaking, as far from their "suns," in their infinitely small
way, as we are from our Sun.

My kingdom is not of this world *(John 18:36)*. If it
were, what a kingdom it would be. It would be on a par with
the kingdom of Cyrus, Alexander, Caesar, Napoleon, the
German Kaiser, and so on. Yet, the Christian world believes
that the one who made that statement, will return to Earth,
"with his saints," take up the royal scepter, and "reign a
thousand years" *(Revelation 20:5)*. This is the belief of the
millennia lists, of whom there are millions.

The "Kingdom of God" is not restricted to the tiny globe
on which we live. It includes the vast space in which are
floating planets so large that the comparison of them to our
Earth sinks our Earth into the insignificance of a grain of
sand. It includes space so vast that the endless flight of Time
can never encompass it. And it includes space so small, that
the microscope cannot reveal it.

To enter the spiritual world or "heaven" as it is called, requires no long journey. Man from the first, as we have seen,
is an inhabitant of it. Wherever there are material substances,
there likewise is the spiritual world. In other words, the
material world beheld by us is a manifestation of an invisible
spiritual world. The visible world, as we have seen in the Law
of Change, issues from and returns to the invisible world
daily and hourly. "Above" the Earth, and "below" it, are
conditions that are changing every moment.

The blue, radiant, infinite sky is the material emblem
beyond which heaven was said to be. But we are learning that
heaven does not lie in space, because it does not belong to
space. *That is the very letter of Scripture.* "The kingdom of

God is within you" — therefore were you carried to the most distant star, you should be not a step nearer the kingdom of God than at this moment.

It is only the materialist who believes in a distant heaven. Heaven, like the atmosphere, is at once quite close and far away. It is as near to our "soul," as our "soul" is to our body; and it is as far from our body as our body is from our "soul" —so near that they intermingle, and so far apart that nothing can bridge the intervening chasm.

At death, so-called, there is no migration of the "soul" to some distant shore. The road to our eternal home is simply a casting off of the material frame — for flesh and blood cannot inherit it *(1 Corinthians 5:50)*.

This explains the "born again" mystery. Verily, verily, I say unto thee, except a man be born again, he cannot see the kingdom of God *(John 3:3)*. And Verily, verily, I say unto you, He that hearth my word, and believeth on him that sent me, hath (now) everlasting life, and shall not come into condemnation (death); but is passed (now) from death unto life *(John 5:24)*.

Not the slightest inference of a long journey to the "heavenly home" can be gathered from the letter or from the spirit of these expressions.

What are the landscape features of that land of paradise, of course we cannot know till it we enter; "neither hath it entered into the heart of man to conceive." But the inspiration that promises it, says also that the invisible things of Him are clearly seen by the things which are made — signifying that the splendors of futurity, though in their fullness unimaginable, are nevertheless pictured in those of the visible realm.

The great trouble with every man is, that he is never satisfied with his present state of life. He can see romance and beauty and pleasure only in the things that lie far removed from him. While on earth, he despises it, slanders it, fixes his eyes on its gloom, and forgets its glory.

While here, the living should see the matchless beauty of the Creator's handiwork, should belong to this life, and live in this life; and not neglect it, and attempt to live in the life to come. The only way to serve the Creator is to obey His law, and this we are not doing when we live as we see man now living.

Anything that too powerfully attracts us away from the duties of the present life, cannot be regarded as beneficial, and the Creator never intended for it to be that way. The Creator has shown us that it is His will that we should not do so, by withholding from us every clue as to the time of our departure, and all knowledge of our destination.

# Chapter No. 37
# Dust Returns to the Ground

Cursed is the ground for thy sake; in sorrow shalt thou eat of it all the days of thy life; thorns and also thistles shall it bring forth to thee; and thou shalt eat the herb of the fields; in the sweat of thy face shalt thou eat bread, till thou return unto the ground; for out of it was thou taken: for dust thou art, and unto dust shalt thou return. *(Genesis 3:17-19)*.

Notwithstanding the specificness of the above statements, there is and has always been much and varied speculation as to what is here really meant, and what becomes of man after death. No positive, universal conclusion has been reached in regard to the proposition. But so far as the physical part of man is concerned, the question was clearly settled many centuries ago.

The body of man was taken from the dust of the ground. That statement is not a mere figure of speech; it is an actual, literal fact. Every visible form or structure on earth, has been produced from the air, sunshine, water, and soil. Every plant, shrub, tree, and animal, which has been or may hereafter be, is only a definite form that has been constructed by Divine Life out of the surrounding environment. There is, in fact, no other source from which these forms can come.

But here again man is loathed to believe that what befalleth the beasts, also befalleth men. Yet the Preacher, the son of David, king in Jerusalem, King Solomon in other words, declared that this is true. He says:

1 - For that which befalleth the sons of men befalleth beasts;
2 - even one thing befalleth them;
3 - as the one dieth, so dieth the other;
4 - yea, they have all one breath;
5 - so that a man hath no preeminence above a beast (in death);

6 - all go unto one place;

7 - all are of the dust,

8 - and all turn to dust again *(Ecclesiastes 3:19-20).*

He then challenged any one to show him wherein he was wrong. He asks:

1 - Who knoweth the spirit of man that goeth upward;

2 - and the spirit of the beast that goeth downward to the earth?

*"All life is an expression of the Divine Life,"* says the Oriental sage. The expression of that may be through plant, animal or man, yet it is the expression of the Divine Life through a form composed of the dust of the ground.

Divine Life, guided by Infinite Intelligence, brings together into definite relationship, from the air, sunshine, water, and soil, certain elements or materials, constructs these into various forms, through which Divine Life operates in the performance of specific purposes. This fact was known to Moses.

The material form of man depends for its organized and animated existence upon Divine Life flowing through it. This state continues as long as Divine Life can control the material form, and ends when that control is lost. However, it is not exactly correct to state that Divine Life loses control of matter, for matter is always under control. But when the organized body becomes so abnormal that it does not comply with the law which governs the operation of Divine Life in and through it, Divine Life withdraws from the body, and the body lapses back into the motionless state, called death.

When the death penalty was passed upon man, it affected the whole man and not part of him. But it affected only the material part and not the spiritual part, for the spiritual part is the Divine Life. Man was made of material substance. All these is to man is of the earth, earthy. He is a material form that receives an influx of life from the Divine Life and it is the material form only that returns to the ground.

When the Divine Life withdraws from the material body, all function at once comes to an end, for the function of the body and all its parts arises as a result of the Divine Life flowing in and through the body, just as the function of a steam engine depends upon the steam flowing through it.

At this point science again makes a terrible error. The findings of all biologists and physiologists are based upon the assumption that life is inherent in animal bodies. They believe that a body functions because it functions, and that this function arises from certain chemical actions and reactions occurring in the body. Whereas, the body functions because it is enlivened and quickened with the Divine Life.

Since the material form of man depends absolutely for its organized existence upon Divine Life, when Divine Life departs from the material form, the process of disintegration instantly begins, and, by virtue of the work of certain animated forms, termed bacteria or germs, placed on earth for a particular purpose, and never varying in the least from that path, the material form is soon dissolved back into the unorganized state, and there comes to pass the saying that is written:

Then shall the dust return to the earth as it was *(Ecclesiastes 12:7)*.

As Grindon so beautifully puts it:

"Life winds its little circles, hour by hour, day by day, year by year, faithfully concluding every ring before another is begun, but never failing to commence afresh where it left off, and so goes on everlastingly, ring rising upon ring, every circle covering and reiterating its predecessors, on a higher level, nearer and nearer to the heavens. The material body drops away, like dead leaves, but Life goes on, in beautiful and ceaseless aspiration."

Fichte observes:

"All death in nature is life, and in death appears visibly the advancement of life. It is not death which kills, but the higher life, which, concealed behind the other, begins to develop itself. Death and birth are but the struggle of Life with itself to attain a higher form" (*Destination of Man,* page 127).

Technically speaking, even the motionless form of clay, after the departure of the Life Principle, is not absolutely dead, for Grindon writes:

"Every atom of the constituent matter of our globe is alive. 'Inanimate matter,' 'dead matter,' often vaguely spoken of, matter waiting for the breath of Ditty to give it life, does not exist. Matter is not a hearth existing anteriorily to life, and independently of life, and upon which the flame of life is kindled. In its very simplest and crudest forms it is a sign that the flame is already burning."

The body, therefore, is not absolutely dead, but relatively so. It is true that it dissolves and returns to dust, as we are told, just as all material forms have done since the world began. But it does not pass from the plane of use, any more than does the material form of a horse or a hog. Why should it? Is man not born like a wild ass's colt *(Job 11:12)?*

The dissolved material form of man, being returned to its original inorganic elements, is utilized again in the evolution of other forms; for it becomes the fertile soil, as it was before, out of which come forth again plants, shrubs, trees, animals, and men, just as has been taking place from the first.

The poets have sung this song for numberless generations, and come close to the truth, yet without a single thought, perhaps, of the fact. This is well illustrated in the philosophical lines of Pope, who wrote:

*And life dissolving, vegetates again;*
*All forms that perish other forms supply —*
*showing how truly —*
*States fall, Arts fade, but Nature does not die*
*and vividly portraying that —*
*All are but parts of one stupendous whole,*
*Whose body Nature is, and God the soul.*

But Pope fell into the same error that has always beset the leaders of men. He believed that it was "life" which dissolved and vegetated again. This is only a half-truth; and it is these half-truths which appear so plausible, which have led the best men astray, and which have done most of the damage that has been inflicted upon the race. It is the material form only that dissolves, and returns to dust.

# Chapter No. 38
# Spirit Returns To The Creator

God is a Spirit *(John 4:24)*. That, which is born of the Spirit, is spirit *(John 3:6)*. We dwell in Him, and He in us, because He hath given us of His Spirit *(1 John 4:13)*. In that day ye shall know that ye are in Me, and I in you *(John 14:20)*.

The wind bloweth where it listeth, and thou hearest the sound thereof, but canst not tell whence it cometh, and whither it goeth: so is every one that is born of the Spirit *(John 3:8)*.

And it is written that, Except a man be born of the Spirit, he cannot enter the kingdom of God *(John 3:5)*, Again, It is the spirit that quickeneth; the flesh profited nothing *(John 6:63)*.

Putting these statements together, we observe that man is told over and over again, that what appears to be his life is really The Great Spirit expressing itself on the visible plane. For it is The Spirit that animates the flesh, while the flesh profits nothing.

By this we know that what appears to be the life of man, is born of the Spirit; and being born of the Spirit, the spiritual-part, the living-part, of man, which is Life, is capable of entering "the kingdom of God," while the material-part of man, the earthy-part, the dead-part, "profiteths nothing," but at death, as we by habit call that state, the material-part returns to the material (earth) as it was.

However, it would not be very conducive to the interest of the church to explain so clearly and simply these apparently great mysteries. For we must not forget that the church has worldly interests to protect as well as other commercial institutions. For this reason, it has clothed religion with as much twaddle and bunk as medicine was wrapped around the subject of disease — and for the same purpose.

The origin of the false idea of the so-called soul's sinking into a state of torpor after what we call death is easily accounted for. Like all other falsities in psychology and theology, it comes of false physiology, and is directly traceable to the materialistic theory that Life is the fumes (flame) generated by decaying matter. This preposterous thought regards the body as a lamp which gives off a flame, and when the body ceases to function, the flame dies and disappears

Based on this theory, we have Life arising as a mere function of the body, the corollary of which is, that there is no visible organization but that of matter, therefore, matter is essential to Life, and thus when the body ceases to function, in the state we call death, theology teaches that the so-called soul collapses into an insensate, motionless, incompetent nothing, so to remain till re-clothed with "flesh and blood" at the "great judgment day." Such teaching may save the church, but it will never save humanity.

Man is believed to be a living, thinking, acting creature. And so he is, but not of himself, not of his material body. He is a living, thinking, acting being because of his Spiritual Body, about which the poets of all ages have sung such sweet songs. From the first moment of his existence, he is, as we are taught in the Scriptures, an inhabitant of the natural (material-visible-temporal) world, and just as truly of the Spiritual (invisible-eternal) World. Nothing could be plainer than the various unequivocal, un-contradictory statements made as to this.

Materialists hold that the brain produces life, as the liver produces bile and as the stomach produces gastric juice. But if Life is the product of matter, how came Life into existence, when matter was motionless, and therefore helpless to produce anything? Life is the cause of organization; Life constructs organized forms; Life transcends organized forms; Life precedes organized forms. And Life survives the destruction of organized forms, since the existence of Life is in no way dependent on organized forms. It existed before organized forms came into being; and it continues after they pass on and return to dust.

If Life were but the activity of the body, simply a "mode of motion," transformed from other motions or forces, and all of man's thoughts and feelings were but new forms of the "continuous adjustment of internal relations to external relations," then when the motion of the "first man," which "is of the earth, earthy," came to an end, the end of the "second man," which "is the Lord from heaven," would also be at hand. But we observe that Life is not part of the body, but distinct from it. Life constructs the organized form, but is different from it.

Neither do the wear and tear of the body affect its Builder any more than the wear and tear of the violin affect the performer. It simply affects the work done. When the violin finally gives way and falls apart, its destruction does not produce the destruction of the performer. The performer does not die because the violin dies. When the body disintegrates and returns to dust, that condition has no more effect on the Mysterious Builder, than does the death of the violin have on the performer.

In chapter ten we saw the Spiritual and the Material unite to form what we called a "new person." From the "clear field," we beheld the granules begin to appear, and, lo, the granules acted in conformity with the "law of a new energy."

The "new energy" was the Spiritual Man — the Potter. The granules were the material man — the Clay.

The "new energy" forms or builds the "new person" of particles taken from the material world, the storehouse of Nature, and maintains the "new person" throughout life to the instant of death. It builds the invisible speck into a 150-pound man; and it departs from the "new person" when conditions become such that it can remain in the "new person" no longer.

Where does the "new energy," the Divine Life, go when it departs from the material form? That question was answered almost three thousand years ago, as follows:

*Then shall the dust return to the earth as it was; and the spirit shall return unto God who gave it (Ecclesiastes 12:7).*

And nothing herein can be construed as contradictory in the least to that statement.

When Life leaves the body, it returns to the same place that it came from? Where did it come from? From nowhere, because it is everywhere omnipresent. If Life is omnipresent, if Life is everywhere always and at the same time, why shall we say that it comes and goes? The expression of Life comes and goes as the forms through which the expression occurs "live and die." But Life cannot come and go when it has no place to come from and no place to go to. We simply think that it comes and goes, just as we think that the Sun rises and sets. As a man thinketh in his heart, so is he. Our thoughts make us, but they do not make true the things about which we think.

Furthermore, why shall we think that Divine Life undergoes any change in status or station, because it builds a tiny speck of colorless colloid into a full-grown man, animates and maintains the form for a time, then departs from that form? Why shall we think that Life must go somewhere, to some mysterious, faraway, unknown place, to some high heaven or lowly hell, because it abides in and animates our body for a number of years?

Why, we so think because it is the absurd teaching of an idolatrous religion. This is the theory taught by a religion, the roots of which run back and draw nourishment from the morbid mind that murdered men who did not believe in it, and defied it. Can good come from such religion? Can truth come from error? Can the leopard change its spots? Can a clean thing come out of an unclean *(Job 14:4)?*

At no time throughout man's living existence, is there the slightest change in the relationship between the "new energy" and the "new person." From the first signs of life in the mother's womb to the instant of death, the relationship existing between the "new energy" and the "new person," between the Spiritual Man and the Physical Man, between Divine Life and Matter, is exactly and precisely the same. This fact is so clear that the Master was much perplexed when, upon His explaining it, His disciples failed to comprehend it.

# Chapter No. 39
# The World Of The Dead

Is there a world of the dead? There is to us, if we so believe. There is nothing good or bad, but thinking makes it (seem) so (Shakespeare). There is nothing living or dead, but thinking makes it seem so. And as a man thinketh in his heart, so is he.

There are millions now living that shall never see death. And whosoever liveth and believeth in me shall never die. Verily, verily, I say unto you, He that believeth on me hath (now) everlasting life. Verily, verily, I say unto you, If a man keep my saying, he shall never see death. Verily, verily, I say unto you, He that heareth my word, and believeth on him that sent me, hath (now) everlasting life, and shall not come into condemnation (death); but is passed (now) from death (condemnation) unto life (*John 5:24, and 6:47; and 8:51; and 11:26).*

No statements could be more broad and comprehensive than these. And the tense is present — man hath now everlasting life, if he hearth my word, and believeth that he is, because the Father is. If a man believeth that he liveth because the Great Spirit quickens his flesh, such man hath (now) everlasting life.

What is death? What do we mean when we speak of a man's being dead? We generally understand that he has "lost his life." But did he have a "life" to lost? Is it not a case of false belief? He *thought* he had a "life" to lose, and lost what he *thought* he had. And he *thought* he had a "life" because he did not understand the teaching of Christ, and therefore knew not what "life" is.

What is death? That depends upon what Life is; Paul says that "to be carnally minded is death." To be carnally minded means to be limited in one understands of Life. If we believe that a man is dead when all functions of the body stop, we are carnally minded, and, to us, such man is dead. But this is a delusion. We think he is dead because we do not know what Life is, and our thinking makes it seem so to us.

Let us consider the subject from another angle. What is darkness? Is it anything in itself? Is there any darkness to the bat, the cat, the rabbit, or the owl? Since these creatures can see as well or better at night than we can in daytime, how then can we claim that there is darkness?

To a blind-man there is no light. To him there is nothing but darkness. To us there is darkness only at night; and to the owl there is never any darkness. Thus we observe that the condition of darkness, so-called, does not exist except in the mind. There is really no darkness.

In the vast depths of the sea, fishes are that have no eyes. To them there is only darkness. Suppose that we should find ourselves in a world of human beings that had no eyes. We could talk for ages to these sightless people about the wonders of the world of vision, but they would never understand the meaning of a single word we spoke. To these people of darkness there is no beauty of sea and sky, no forms of clouds and mountains, no colors of purple and gold, no features and gestures of friends and relatives.

Suppose that to these folks we should describe the beauties and wonders of what we saw. What would they think of our statements? They could not understand us; they would not believe in us. To them there is no world of vision, and to them our words have no meaning.

This is a hard saying; who can hear it *(John 6:60)?* We fancy we could hear them say. And they would murmur at it, and we would ask, doth this offend you *(John 6:61)* Because I tell you the truth, ye believe me not *(John 8:45)* And we would not be surprised if they went back, and walked no more with us *(John 6:66).*

If a man is deaf, to him there is no world of sound. We could talk to him of the charm of music, the rhythm of the babbling brook, the song of the mocking-bird, but he could not comprehend the meaning of our words, for he could not even hear our words. He is dead so far as the world of sound is concerned. Likewise, to the blind, there is no world of vision. They are also dead so far as the world of vision is concerned.

Those who are carnally minded are dead so far as the World of Life, the Spiritual World, is concerned. When Christ discoursed on the Spiritual World, when he spoke to the carnally minded multitude the marvelous words of "spirit and of life," they could not understand. They knew nothing about Life; they were dead so far as the World of Life was concerned. They thought they were life, that beyond their own body their life did not extend; and so the Master's words found no responsive chord in their material hearts. They could not comprehend the meaning of his words when he said, He that hearth my word hath everlasting life — he is passed out of death into life — here and now.

Even then they were dead, and knew it not. Whereas, by understanding his word, they would have passed from death into life, there and then.

Death is the king of terrors. It is a word that seems to define a condition which all men dread to meet. But when rightly viewed, the word grows exceedingly weak; it loses its force, and vanishes into nothing before truth, just as darkness disappears before a clear understanding.

If we desire to rise above "the word of the dead," we must become spiritually minded; and when we rise to that plane of understanding, all mystery vanishes, and we come into the light of truth.

Twenty-five hundred years ago, in Athens, the greatest teacher of his day was waiting for the hour of sunset. At the moment when the sun seemed to touch the horizon, he was condemned to drain the cup of hemlock and then lie down to die. His disciples gathered around him for a final conversation. They asked him where he wished to be buried. And the martyr made answer in words that have become immortal:

*"You may bury me — if you can catch me."*

Such are they that are born of the spirit. Thou canst not tell whence it cometh and whither it goeth. This is the quality of Life. Search for it not; neither believe that you are Life.

When Socrates spoke thus to his troubled disciples, he spoke not only for himself, but for all humanity. He voiced the universal instinct that is found in every breast. *Man does not die — he goes.*

There can be no death unless there be something to die. The material body is not alive, so it can not die. And since there is only One Life, and that is Divine Life, and since Divine Life is eternal and everlasting, without beginning and without end, how can what we call "death" have existence, except in the imagination?

The world of darkness exists only in fancy to the blind. The world of the dead exists only in fancy to the carnally minded. The carnally minded think there is a world of the living, and also a world of the dead — and it is their thinking only that makes it seem so. Beyond the limits of their thoughts and imagination, there are no such worlds, states, or conditions.

# Chapter No. 40
# This is Life Eternal

Verily, verily, I say unto thee, except a man be born again, he cannot see the kingdom of God *(John 3:3)*. For flesh and blood cannot inherit it *(1 Corinthians 15:50)*. That which is born of the flesh is flesh; and that which is born of the Spirit is spirit *(John 3:6)*.

There is a natural body, and there is a spiritual body. That was not first which is spiritual, but that which is natural; and afterward that which is spiritual. The first man is of the earth, earthy: the second man is the Lord from heaven *(1 Corinthians 15:44-46-47)*.

Marvel not that I said unto thee, Ye must be born again. The wind bloweth where it listeth, and thou hearest the sound thereof, but canst not tell whence it cometh, and whither it goeth: so is every one that is born of the Spirit *(John 3:7-8)*.

We observe that a man is born twice: of the flesh, and of the spirit; and that when man is born of the spirit it is called the second birth — the "born again" proposition which gives much mystery to material religion. And we observe that the second birth, the spiritual birth, is "the Lord from Heaven."

He that cometh from above is above all: he that is of the earth is earthy, and speaketh of the earth *(John 3:31)*. The material religionist speaks in material terms, and is of the earth, earthy; and therefore knows nothing of the spiritual part of him, that comes from above.

Verily, verily, I say unto you, He that heareth my word, and believeth on him that sent me, hath (now) everlasting life, and is passed (now) from death unto life. Verily, verily, I say unto you, the hour is coming, and now is, when the dead shall hear the voice of the Son of God: and they that hear shall live *(John 5:24-25)*.

The dead are they that are lost; and they that are lost are they that think they are life, and that they have life in themselves. But they are dead; for they have no life; they are of the earth, earthy; they are born of the flesh and are flesh. But they know not that they are born of the spirit, and therefore the belief that the Father alone hath life in Himself is not in them *(John 5:26)*.

Life is not an observed reality; it is an invisible potency, comprehended in the mind of him only that lives by faith. The source of Life is the Creator, the common Father, not only of man, but of all creation. He is the Father that hath life in Himself.

Life is a Force of Infinite Intelligence, so far as we can know, which operates in and through the material body in the performance of certain work. Life is not function, process, nor product; it is the CAUSE of all these. Life is not the product of earth, air, and water. These are the materials out of which Life constructs visible forms, under the directing Law of the Universe.

Man is not life; man is not alive. His living existence is nothing more nor less than the result of Divine Life flowing through his body. All the functions and processes of his body, regardless of what they may be, or of what biologists and physiologists say of them, are produced by Divine Life; for apart from Divine Life, the body is dead — is a motionless mass of clay.

Mind is one phase of the function, of the body produced by Divine Life. And it is the primary one, since through the mind only can man conceive of his relationship to his Creator, his Father. As false belief and false teaching led him astray, he failed to understand the messages transmitted to him by Divine Life through his mind, and he believed that he was life, and became lost.

When men rise up, cast off false belief and false teaching, rend the veil that hides the light, and discover their relationship to the Father, and teach that doctrine to a lost world, they are promptly burned and crucified. For to know the truth is to be set free from the galling yoke of sects, creeds, and chains, and this course is dangerous for religions, rulers and leaders *(John 8:32)*.

If we let him thus alone, all men will believe on him. And Caiaphas, the high priest, said unto them, Ye know nothing at all, nor consider that it is expedient for us, that one man should die for the people, and that the whole nation perish not *(John 11:48-49-50)*. And so men continue to remain lost in their false thoughts and teachings, and to wander in the darkness of superstition and ignorance.

Since Life is not in nor from Nature, then Life cannot be temporal, for temporal things are such as are proper to Nature. From this we know that Life is eternal, for the Creator alone is Life, and so Life is without limit and without end.

Nothing can proceed from anyone except what is in him. Since the Creator is infinite and Eternal, these qualities only can come from Him. The Infinite cannot proceed from the Finite; yet the Infinite appears to proceed from the Finite; but this is from appearance only. For the Infinite proceeds through the Finite, and not from the Finite. Eternity inheres in the so-called soul of man, by virtue of the "Breath of Life" that man, received in the beginning, when he was born of The Spirit. Through The Spirit man was to know Him, the Father for — THIS IS LIFE ETERNAL, THAT THEY MIGHT KNOW THEE THE ONLY TRUE GOD *(John 17:3)*.

Death is not a reality, but a belief. And the belief that man dies is based on a false conception of what Life is. Man is not Life, therefore man cannot die, since man never lived.

When Life leaves the body, the body loses all appearance of being alive, and by habit based on false belief, we say that such a body is dead. The truth is, the body never lived — it was only quickened by the spirit; the flesh profited nothing. The flesh never lived, therefore the flesh never died.

A man appears to die when the Spiritual Man departs from the material man. This is not death except in the imagination of him only who thinks that he is Life, and that Life dies. He who has found the Father, knows that Life is Spirit, and that Spirit is the only true God, and knowing this, likewise knows that he cannot die. Therefore —

Whosoever liveth and believeth in me shall never die. And he that believeth in me, though he were dead, yet shall he live *(John 11:25-26)*.

Just what meaning do these words convey? Christ teaches the relationship between God and man from the first. And the fundamental fact taught in Genesis is, that Life is God and that God is Life. Christ, seeing that the world did not understand, endeavored to impress that truth upon man in this remarkable statement:

God is a Spirit *(John 4:24)*. It is the spirit that quickeneth; the flesh profited nothing: the words that I speak unto you, they are spirit, and they are life *(John (6:63)*.

And again he says: I live by the Father *(John 6:57)*.

Christ not only knew what Life is, but by these words he declared that his material form, like that of everything that liveth, was quickened by the spirit, and had no life in itself. He declared that he lived because there flowed through his body, the Life of the one common Father of all living things. But how was he to get this truth through the steel armor of false belief and false teaching that still encompasses the mind of man? He tried it in many ways, and by many proverbs, parables, allegories, and symbols. He implored men to believe in him, in his word, in his teaching. He says: Except ye eat the flesh of the Son of man, and drink his blood, ye have no life in you. Whoso eateth my flesh, and drinketh my blood, hath eternal life (now); and I will raise him up at the last day (the day he thinks he dies) *(John 6:53-54)*.

And again:

Verily, verily, I say unto you, if a man keep my saying, he shall never see death *(John 8:51)*.

What are his sayings? That there is only one true God, that God is a Spirit, that the Spirit quickeneth the body, and that to know this is here and now LIFE ETERNAL. That is the flesh he wants men to eat, and the blood he urges them to drink, and the word he implores them to believe when he declares: Verify, verily, I say unto you, He that believeth on me hath (now) everlasting life *(John 6:47)*.

For he that believeth, while he liveth, that his body is not alive, but is quickened by the Great Spirit, and believeth that all the power his body expresses is the effect of the Great Spirit flowing in and through it, knows that his apparent Life, which is the Great Spirit, cannot die, and, consequently, though his body be dead, yet he lives and knows that he lives. But this can be understood only by those men of broad minds who can grasp the final analysis of what Life is.

Why is a definite statement made here as to THE ONLY TRUE GOD? We must recollect that the ancients had many and various gods. That is why a specific distinction is made in the phrase, THE ONLY TRUE GOD. There is only one TRUE GOD, and if we knew THE ONLY TRUE GOD, by reason of that fact alone we know what Life is — for THE ONLY TRUE GOD is all Life, and all Life is THE ONLY TRUE GOD.

Hence, to know that God is Life is to know that Life is God, and by this knowledge we know THE ONLY TRUE GOD. And to know THE ONLY TRUE GOD is to know that Life, which animates our material form, is LIFE ETERNAL.

This is the whole sum and substance of the teachings of Christ. Not once did He mean to convey any information that could be construed as relating to material things. When He spoke, it was of the Spiritual, which He was forced to describe and define in material terms. Nevertheless, The words that I speak unto you, they are spirit and they are life. And verily, verily, I say unto you, If a man keep my sayings, he shall never see death *(John 6:63; 8:31)*.

Man's Life IS eternal; not TO BE eternal. The dust returns to the earth as it was; but the Spirit (God-Life-Soul) returns to the Source whence it came. Life runs into eternity, partitioned from it only by a thin, dissolving veil of flesh (dust), constructed from the material world. Time is simply that part of Eternity in which Life operates through the material form.

Life is simply one phase of the everlasting and eternal I AM; and those who understand the teaching of Jesus, also understand this, and, as He so often said, will never see death. For death is but a belief, an illusion known to those only who hearing cannot understand. Those who cannot understand will see death only because they so believe. They will die in the thought that Life can die. As a man thinketh in his heart, so is he. It is our thoughts that rule us. We die because we think we die, and not because we die.

Man does not live as a material being, die as a material being, and come to life again as a spiritual being. He is the image of the Creator, not in matter, but in Spirit. What we call Life is the Living Spirit, expressing through matter (man) the VISIBLE PRESENCE OF THE GREAT I AM. Here is the Living God, abiding in His Kingdom, located within the Temple, which Temple ye are!

The big question of the ages is, "If a man die, shall he live again" *(Job 14:14)*.

THERE IS NO DEATH declared the Ancient Masters five thousand years ago. We are deceived by our sight. "There is no Death! What seems so is transition. This life of Mortal Breath is but a suburb of the Life Elysian, whose portal we call Death" — *Longfellow*.

Professor Hotema unfolds the Cosmic Cycle of Eternal Life, taught by the Masters five thousand years ago as stated, and was common knowledge until the 4th Century A.D., when a terrible event occurred that changed the history of all countries controlled by the Roman Empire, blotting out Ancient Wisdom and plunging Europe into a pit of darkness that lasted for more than a thousand years, as explained in *The Soul's Secret*.

The World Within reverts to the Ancient Wisdom which taught the Kingdom of Life is within *(Luke 17:21)*. Lost is he who looks without for substance with which to improve the Kingdom of Life Within. This makes worthless the institution of medical art. All creatures below man have no use for its products, and as they are ruled by the same law that governs man, it is logical that he also has no use for them.

The Last book of the Bible deals allegorically with the Kingdom of Life Within. The Book With Seven Seals *(Revelation 5)* is man's body. Its Seven Vital Control Centers are called Seals because in the average individual they are in a semi-dormant state, which reduces Consciousness to a very low level. These Control Centers were called Chakras by the Hindu Masters, and are located in the body as shown in the picture here. They are numbered from the bottom up, the 6th and 7th being located in the brain.

Here the Masters are presenting certain functions of the organism relative to its Creative Power. They discovered that when this Power is diverted from its procreative function, it produces amazing effects that are highly beneficial to the organism, and, when controlled and guided, activates the Seven Centers mentioned, resulting in a surprising increase in Consciousness that makes such man a Seer.

That is the reason why the Masters guarded this discovery with such great care, imparting the secret only to the Neophyte in the Ritual of Initiation in the Ancient Mysteries. That is the story allegorically related in

Revelation. We shall notice some of it: — "And I saw heaven (sky) opened, and Behold! a white horse (appeared); and he that sat upon him was called Believable and True, and with justice he judges and gives battle. His eyes were as a Flame of Fire, and on his head were many diadems; and (on his forehead) he had written a name that no man. knew save himself. And he was clothed with a vesture dipped in blood; and his name is called the SON OF LIGHT" — *Revelation 19:11-13.*

The Hero on the white horse is the Initiate. He is now the Conqueror  who, by indomitable will, has finished the elastic work of Initiation in the Ancient Mysteries, and is no longer the common Man of Darkness. On his head was placed the Triple Crown to indicate his status as an Initiate, he was clad in a garment dyed red, and called Son of Light.

Revelation is one of the most stupendous allegories ever written. It is the story of the sensations of the Neophyte as he passed through the Ritual of Initiation in the Ancient Mysteries. The tale is told in terms of creative phenomena. The Hero is the Sun, the Heroine the Moon, and all other characters are Planets, Stars, and Constellations. Its stage-setting comprises Sky, Earth, Rivers and Sea. It elucidates its subject with the glare of lightning, proclaims it with the roll of thunder, emphasizes it with the shock of the earthquake, and reiterates it with the Ocean's voice, the ceaseless murmur of its "many waters." Ever it maintains this cosmic terminology, this vast phrasing of CREATION. In the first chorus of Constellations which encircle the throne of the Sun-God, the starry hosts praise him as the Creator of the Universe. But when the drama has been enacted, that Universe has perished, "the first sky and the first earth were passed away, and the sea exists no more." Then from his throne the Sun-God announces "Behold! I make all things new."

THIS IS REGENERATION. This Apocalyptic Universe is Man, the Lesser Cosmos, of whom the Sun-God is really the Architect and Builder, and whom the Moon and all the Stars of the Sky have helped to mold and make.

For in every man, however fallen and degraded, are presented all the forces, both cosmic and deific, that brought him into existence and nurtured him throughout the vast cycles of generation, while his Conscience has taught him the lessons of the Good and True, and the Power of Darkness has held before him the degrading lessons of the Evil and False. These same Cosmic Forces of the Great Creative Principle but await the time when the resurgent Divine Life again stirs within him, and then, disintegrating the elements composing the carnal man, they begin a new evolution, the work of perfect ionizing this Child of the aeons, whom "the Scorpion-monster of Darkness" can drag down till he is lower than the beast, but whom the Creative Principle, the Eagle of Light, can exalt high above the Earth.

## Ancient Secret of Personal Power: Tetragrammation

Good Health is the very foundation of Success. And we have heard health is man's birthright. That is another grievous error. Good health is the reward received by him who earns it. Contents: *Kingdom within, Perfection is within, Secrets of the Body, Mysterious Glands, Seven Astral Centers, Tetragrammation, Science of Sensology, Edocrinology, Higher Consciousness, Theology, Seership, Astral Light, Living Fire, Macrocosm, Time-Eternity.*

## Ancient Sun God

Contents: *The Ancient Light, The Great Sun God, Secret of the Stars, Astrology Changed to Astronomy, Virgin Mother, Majesty of God's Kingdom, The Sovereign Sun, Ab-Ram the Sun-God, Lamb of God, Perfection.*

## Awaken the World Within

Contents: The Course of Study, 58 wonderful lessons. *These lessons show how the higher faculties of mind and soul may be aroused and activated, thus enabling the body, through which the real man contacts the physical plane, to express the noblest characteristics. If you are seeking the highest spheres of mental, physical existence, you should find in these lessons the help and guidance you need.*

## Cosmic Science of the Ancient Masters

Contents: *If a man die, shall he live again? Is reincarnation a fact? The sublime truths of the Universe. The Mysteries of Nature, of Man; The Grand Cycle of Creation, Conscious & Subconscious Mind, Intuition, Immorality, Dormant Organs, The Mysterious Chambers in the Skull.* Highly Illustrated with rare Occult Illustrations.

## The Kingdom of Heaven

Contents: *The Grand Cosmic Kingdom and its Seven Parts. The Mental Kingdom; Consciousness and Super-consciousness; Why People Fail; Freedom and Slavery; The Spiritual Organs and Powers; The State of Brahma; Telepathy and Television; The Fourth Dimension.*

## Living Fire or God's Law of Life

Contents: *The Ageless Wisdom of the Ancient masters tells us that the Divine Trinity is reflected in man, and his Knowledge, when correctly and clearly interpreted as Hotema has presented it in his various works, will lift the veil that darkens the Mind and reveal to the understanding of man the facts of Eternal Life.*

# The Magic Wand

Contents: *The Serpentine Fire, its energizing through the subtle body centers (chakras): Mastery over the senses; Awakening of the 6th and 7th senses; The Black and White Serpent; The Golden Oil of Kanda; Biblical truths that have been Suppressed.*

# The Magic World

Hotema tells a private story about himself that he has never before told in his writings. Contents: *Magic Intelligence, Magic World, Magic Esotericism, Magic and Mystery, Magic Creation, Magic Message, Magic Spirit, Magic Kingdom, Magic Wires, Magic Sensology, Magic Chambers, The Magician, Magic Light, Magic Attraction, Magic Mate, Magic Practice, Magic End.*

# Man's Higher Consciousness

Contents: *The author claims this work shows the reason why the radio and television mechanism in the human skull fails to respond fully now to cosmic radiation as it did twenty thousand years ago, when the Ancient Masters accumulated their wisdom of Creation, Life and Man, then recorded it in fable and fiction, for interpretation to those who proved by test they were worthy to receive the same. The author covers subjects such as daily exercise, vegetarian diet, raw foods, sunbathing, periodical fasting, deep breathing, history of longevity, cosmic forces, secrets of the ancient masters.*

## The Mysterious Sphinx

Contents: *Why is it an object of awe and reverence. A startling expose showing how a symbol for the ancient masters evolved into the God of Christianity. The secret of the Cosmic Principles which Constitute Man; The Lost Word; The Vital Principle of Life; How the Masters Communed with the Cosmic Powers and Principle; How symbolism Develops Man.*

## The Magic Temple (Forthcoming Spring 2019)

Contents: *The amazing powers of the human body. The author says the world is still trying to solve the mystery of man. Is God as described in the first book of the bible? The evolutionists refuse to consider that fabulous account, and assert that man is the product of creation. People grow up in that confusion and know not what to believe. There is no death, as religion teaches. Food does not build blood as science teaches. Food doesn't give nourishment to the body as taught by the dietitians. Man need not die at 100 years. He quotes scores of unusual facts seldom found in the average textbook.*

## The Mystery of Man

Contents: *The cosmic process of transforming solarized man into physical man, Illusions, The dual aspect, The identity of ego, The secret of the atom, Doctrine of numbers.*

## The Facts of Nutrition

Contents: *The variety of the organism depends not on the food and drink, for experience teaches athletes to go into action with empty stomachs. The author gives his concepts that the growth of the body does not result from food consumption, but from the division and subdivision of the parent cell. What food does not and cannot produce, it cannot and does not sustain.*

## The Genesis of Christianity

Contents: *Hilton Hotema started in Sunday School — he went regularly until he was fifteen. At twelve, he began the study of the Bible in earnest. He became a preacher and after preaching in scores of different states and finally found the truth was not being given to the people. He began comparing the various Bible and religious books and found many startling facts which were never given to the people from the pulpit ... never taught in public schools, nor in Sunday Schools. He found the average preacher knew a little about the history of the bible, and was shouting about things that were not true. He discovered why the Roman Empire was plunged into mental darkness with the birth of Christianity. That darkness was necessary to help the priesthood frighten people, to keep the priesthood in high places, and to drive the multitude into the church, for the sake of profit and power. He shows why Moses could not have written the Pentateuch (The first five books of the Bible — the account of his own demise — Deuteronomy 3)*

## The Glorious Resurrection (Forthcoming Spring 2019)

Contents: *Symbolism; Ancient Science; Crucified Saviors; Great Mother of the Gods; Mysterious Resurrection; Birth of Gods; Light; Two Bodies in One; Ancient Terminology; Mystic Sleep; Life Swindle of Mytheography; Unknown Joy of Death; The Future Life; Reincarnation; The Universal Fable.*


## The Golden Dawn

Contents: *Those who mourn the dead will be most interested in this work. The Golden Dawn, sharply gleaming on the distant horizon, denotes the approach of a brighter day in the life of man, the Lord of the whole world earth (Zechariah 4:14). The millions of innocent people, sustained by fear of death, sees the brilliant signs and shudders. For the sign heralds the revival of knowledge that will inform man of the mysteries of creation and liberate his mind from fear of death. Man will learn that he is life, and that life has no beginning and has no ending. What appears as death pertains only to the body and not to life. The body was never alive. It was only the mechanism used by life to perform certain work of creation in the visible world.*


## The Great Law

Contents: *Professor Hotema studied the teachings of the Ancients from hidden and revealed sources for over seventy years. He was a student of many movements and teachings, Rosicrucian, Theosophy, Hindu, Hebrew, Egyptian and Grecian Mysteries, Magian Tradition, Masonry, the Tarot, Arcane Sciences, Hygiene, Vegetarian, and many others of which the world has never heard. He delved into ancient records and gathered scattered and widely separated fragments of truth from the ruins of temples of the Masters who were so far ahead of us in knowledge and wisdom that only the few can interpret their true meaning. And he has interpreted it, boiled it down, condensed it into readily comprehensible material.*

## The Great Red Dragon

Contents: *Ancient Scriptures, Tree of Life, Thou Shalt Surely Die, Act of Propagation, Coition and Convulsions, Pituitary Tumors, Sin Unto Death, Card 6 Temptation, Woman Appears first, the Degenerate Woman, Man a Degenerate woman, analysis of Homosexuality.*

## The Secret of Regeneration (Book I)

Contents: Some of the 128 Chapters — *Truth, The Dark Ages, Age of Ignorance, Age of the Earth, Age of Man, Sunken Continents, The Antediluvian World, Ancient Cultures, People of Atlantis, Despots and Tyrants, Nineveh and Assyria, The Chaldeans, The Hebrews, Israelites in Egypt, Driven out of Egypt, The Babylonian Captivity, The Scriptures of the Jews, The First Forgery, The Priest and the Scribe, The Second Forgery, The Pentateuch, The Third Forgery, Story of the Exodus, Biblical Contradictions, The Fourth Forgery, The Synoptic Gospels, Many Gospels, The Work of the Priesthood, The Need for Gospels, The Essenes, Pious Fraud, Ecclesiastical Lying and Forgery, Argument Against Christianity, Is Jesus a Myth/ Deceiving the Masses, How the Church Triumphed, etc., etc., etc.*

# The Secret of Regeneration (Book II)

Contents: Some of the 84 Chapters — *Sex Symbols, The Garden of Eden, The Tree of Knowledge, The Serpent, The Sons of God, The Law of Nature, Evolution vs. Devolution, Law of Cause and Effect, The Perfect Man, Degeneration of the Gods, Sex and Seed, Similitude of the Sexes, Rudimentary Organs, Appearance of Woman, Law of Variation, The Hermaphrodite, Amativeness, Sexual Consciousness, Asexuality, Auto-Sexuality, Degradation of Women, Sex in Religion, Morality & the Church, Woman under Church Rule, Traces of Woman Rule, Marriage, Woman the Superior, Is Coition Natural for Men, Coition & Convulsions, The Virgin Mother, Preventing Impregnation Mentally, Fornication & Imagination, Woman Appears First, The Degenerate Woman, Man a Degenerate Woman, Perfect Man Born, Not Made.*

# The Divine Life

Contents: *What is Life, Dust of the Ground, Breath of Life, Law of Creation, Law of Change, Creative Force, Origin of Life, Kinds of Life, Hidden Artist, Man is Not Life, When Man Begins to Live, Relation of Man to Life, Man Does Nothing of Himself, Influence of Tradition, Ancient Worship Rules Today, In Spirit and in Truth, What is the Soul? The Mysterious Force, What is Intuition, Voice of the Soul, Divine Intelligence, Why Men are Mocked, Death Penalty of Disobedience, The Great Commandment, How Long Should Man Live? Fountain of Youth, Human Intellect, Was Man Born to Die, Influence of Suggestion, Conditions of Eternal Life, How old is the Body, From Master to Slave, Where is Hell? Where is Heaven? Doctrine of Atonement,*

*Return to Obedience, Life Eternal, Dust Returns to the Ground, Spirit Returns to the Creator, Life Eternal, World of the Dead.*

## Live Longer

Contents: *Right Living, Healthful Environment, Climate, Man's Home, The Artificial World, The Art of Living, He Lived 370 Years, Law of Change, Fountain of Youth, Man Once Lived 80,000 Years, Self-Denial.*

## Empyreal Sea: How High Do You Climb: Live 1,400 Years

Contents: *The Human Temple, Man Created Perfect, The Aging Process, Secret of Living, The River of Life, The River of Death, Breathing, Eating, Food the Killer, Living Without Eating, Law of Adaption, What is the Empyreal Sea? Search for Longevity, The Perfect Organization, Man's Place in Creation, The Creative Power, The Divine Curse, Marriage, The New Age, Procreation and Expiration, Degeneration.*

## For Orders or More Information Visit/Contact:

## Lushenabook.com

# More Praise For Professor Hilton Hotema

"Your writings have entirely changed my course of thought and so enriched my life that I am eager to read everything you have written and in my consciousness there is a deep sense of gratitude toward you."

— E. Los <u>Angeles, California.</u>
<u> </u>

"I have been reading books on Health and Philosophy for more than 40 years. "May I say that the books written by Professor Hilton Hotema, which I recently purchased from you, are by far the most instructive and the most original I have ever read. I am at a loss for words to give adequate praise to Professor Hotema. Assuring you of my great satisfaction and wishing your company a well-deserved success.

— I remain, <u>L. G. T. Coronado, California."</u>

"I want to express my complete satisfaction for Professor Hilton Hotema's writings, as I find his books very stimulating and educational for sound thinking. Please add the additional books I have selected".

— <u>Thomas Mazucci,</u> New York.

"My wife and I have completed your Hotema Folio (12 books), for the second time. If I could be granted one wish for the greater good for the human race it would be, that every man and woman should read this folio at least once. We have been members of the Rosicrucian Order for many years, and the lessons and instructions covered many of the things in the folio, and prepared our minds for a better understanding."

— George O. Keefer, Los Alamos, New Mexico.

"I have just finished reading *"Man's Higher Consciousness,"* by Professor Hilton Hotema. I think it is a most wonderful book. I think it is the whole truth. I wish I had the information it contains earlier in my life. Many thanks to Professor Hilton Hotema.

— Edmund Groben, Indiana.

"These books have forced me to revise, somewhat reluctantly, of course, a good many of my former 'College degree' ideas about the whole subject of Health. This I am glad to do because now, for the first time I have a clear picture framed in my mind of both the 'beginning and the end' — as it were of what it means to attempt true healing in patients. I would insistently recommend these books to everyone interested in knowing the true facts, especially those whose mission it is to help an ailing Humanity".

— Doctor Amil H. Sprehn, Member
International Society of Naturopathic Physicians.